Reign of a
HUSTLER

NISAA *A.*
SHOWELL

A Life Changing Book in conjunction with Power Play Media
Published by Life Changing Books
P.O. Box 423 Brandywine, MD 20613

Library of Congress Cataloging-in-Publication Data: 2007939105

www.lifechangingbooks.net

ISBN - (10) 1-934230-87-1 (13) 978-1-934230-87-9
Copyright ® 2007

Praises for
Nisaa A. Showell
and
<u>*'Reign of a Hustler'*</u>

"Ms. Showell writes with boldness and clarity, giving the reader
*a visual view of why the seedy obsession of drugs, greed, money, luxury cars,
expensive jewelry, designer clothing and the status of being on top makes this
lifestyle so tempting. Overall, it was an interesting read deeply rooted in the
gangster lifestyle."*

~Kalaani
RAWSISTAZ Reviewers

*"Nisaa I loved your book. I really loved it. Please tell me you're going to
write a sequel to 'The Reign of a Hustler'"*
~JaVonne Briscoe
"One of your Biggest Fans!"

*"Keep your ear to the street and your eyes on this book. Philly's resident tour
guide and newest literary sensation takes you on a journey you won't soon forget."*
~Eric Pete
Author of 'Gets No Love'

*"Nisaa Showell delivers one of this year's most passionate urban love sto-
ries."*
~Simone Says
Readincolor Reviewers

*"I enjoyed reading 'The Reign of a Hustler'. This epic story of love, business
and more love allows the reader to reach a tangible relationship with the
characters and plots. A can't miss, must read!"*
~J. M. Spratley
Morgan State University

In the name of ALLAH
Most Gracious Most Merciful

To Mommy and Daddy whose guidance gave me all that I am. I am nothing without you. My mother received her bachelor and master degrees while raising a family of six children, not including her husband of twenty-nine triumphant years. We broke the sound decibels of LaSalle University's auditorium when the magnificent Rosa Showell made her way across the stage to accept a piece of paper that made it all worth it.

Looking back on one of the saddest days of our lives, she and my brother sat on the steps of what was left of our home after carelessness with fire caused a car to explode behind the house we'd lived in for over a decade. Ironically, the day began with my dad, my sisters, and I having the time of our lives at Dorney Park or maybe it was Hershey. I'd fallen ill on the ride home, which we later learned was a slight case of food poisoning. But all I can remember is the devastating sound of my moms voice, saying 'we don't have no where to live'. She and my brother were asleep inside until by God's grace my grandmother called waking her asking her to come over. Only to return home to ruins.

What followed was the rest of our lives and we still had each other. By the way, we spent the next twenty years in that house and my dad owns it to this day. You may have heard me mention him, Donald Showell. I wish we could share him outside of the family. Say what you will about him but there is no man that will ever be dearer to me. He teaches me well and I say that because I'm learning from him even now. Sorry boys.

We didn't have it all but we always had what we needed. And my sisters can tell you we were the first ones on the block with Nintendo. Seriously, my dad, actually both of my parents have suffered through illness, recent surgeries, rebellious teenagers, and any episode you saw on the Cosby's. But we keep surviving. It is true what they say; the family that prays together really does stay together.

To my beautiful sisters, my brother, and my nieces and

nephews I pray for you more than myself. We've been through, still go through more than anyone can ever imagine. Relief is on the way, I promise.

To my real soldiers, those who ryde and die for me no matters what I don't even have to say anymore.

But I will say this, do what you dream. Know what it means to be honorable. God is real no matter what you call Him. Have some faith. I think we sometimes forget, God is not just there in the bad times, He is there all of the time. Don't just seek His glory in times of need; offer those thanks every waking moment.

But I digress, thank you so much for sitting down with me. I really believe you can be anything you want to be. Be inspired family. By family I mean all of us. We can heal all of this crying if we do the right things collectively. We are one planet, not one country. And we must truly be one people if we hope to survive this outbreak of destruction. That's how I feel even in my sleep.

Please enjoy the entertainment side of the facts. This is my thanks to you. You ready?

Enjoy your ride
Dispatch

Quinnzell Supreme Sharpe

"Damn!!!"

I hung up the phone and slammed it down on the night table. I balled my fists and shook my head in disbelief. I can't believe these dumb mufuckas got shook down again. This got to be like the third time in two months. I might as well be on the strip my damn self. If I didn't know better I would think these niggas were trying to play me. But I know they know the streets, and one well-known fact on the street, don't fuck with me, Quinnzell Supreme Sharpe. My brother DeShawn, De Money Bags on the block, and his team had the Woodland Avenue strip locked since '88. I was a young buck back then, a freshman at West Philadelphia high school, trying to stomp with the big dogs. But De told me he needed me in school so I had to find something in school to keep my interest, because it damn sure wasn't going to be the books.

That's when I started running ball. By the time senior year rolled around in '92, I had led us to two state and one national championship, going for a second that year. Twenty, ten, and five you know how I do. Every college and Big 10 university I could think of was sweating me too crazy. Until, I shattered my knee in the championship. We won regardless, but I couldn't get any school to give me a second glance. I knew my chances of going to college were shot to shit. De said fuck that, that's why we take care of our own and he paid in cash for me to go to Georgetown University. When he dropped me off I told him I wouldn't even try out for the squad. De hugged me and told me to go fuck the academic game up. I knew he was the only person I could always count on. He loved me no matter what and for that I would do anything for him- even die. In '96 when I accepted my bachelors' degree in Business and Accounting it was the first time I saw my brother shed a tear.

When I came into business with him, we started clocking big dollars. I got us into all types of investments. I put money in stocks and I even opened a bank account to stack some loot for later. Business, was and still is booming. Now I have to tell De about these dumb- ass workers. They said it was those two cops, Punk Thomas and Punker Williams. They're always fucking with our strip, looking for a reason to make another young brother the headline for action news at five and six. Shit, at ten and eleven too. But I tell all my workers the same thing; "Never keep your stash on you." That way when the cops roll up you don't have to run because you're not dirty. They can't touch you. Just do what they say. I got lawyers on the payroll just for petty shit like that. Not to mention my high-powered dream team, if shit ever hits the fan. I'm a busy businessman and it's all about the paper chase. Now I have to recoup this paper these workers just got snatched by the cops. With all this extra shit going down I forgot about the smut on her knees in front of me. I looked down to see her pearl shaped head bobbing up and down. No passion, no emotion, just in and out. Honestly, I can't expect any feelings from her because I damn sure don't have any for her. She's just like all the rest of the females from the street. They all know my name ring bells all over. When they meet me they do whatever they can to get my attention and gain my interest. But I need a down ass chick. She got to have her mind right. Independent. Sassy. Classy. She got to keep it gangster. And I'm not hating on the freak jawns, but sucking my dick in my weed crib with my workers downstairs don't get you wifey status.

"Yo, Tiana." I said it real cool so she wouldn't catch feelings about my next move. She peeked up at me.

She took my dick out of her mouth but still stroked him with her hand. She's a dime, but on the real she's a scandalous freak.

More niggas have been in her than jail.

"What's up baby?" she said with a sexy grin on her chocolate face.

Her hair is as short as mine all faded out. Her edges are shaped up shitty sharp with sexy thick eyebrows arched above her scandalous amber eyes.

"I got to make moves right now, but I'm a holla at you later, yamean."

She twisted her face and raised her right eyebrow.

"That's all you wanted me to come in here for?" she asked.

I smiled and stood up. She looked up at me from her position on the floor while I pulled my shit up.

"That's what you came in here for," I said. "What did you say to me when I pulled up on the block Tiana?"

She rolled her eyes.

"I said I was trying to show you something."

"This is what you chose to show me, yamean?"

She bit her bottom lip and put her head down. Silly females put themselves in positions they regret because they don't think about the shit spilling from their lips.

"Stop saying yamean all the time. And when am I going to see you again," she asked facing the floor.

I grinned and shook my head. She done fucked around and fucked up so she feels the need to redeem her woman-hood.

"I'm a hit you up."

Tiana laughed as she got up from the floor. She walked over to the chair and put her jacket on. Damn. Her ass did fit right in those black ENYCE jeans. She got a phat ass, but she ain't really got no body though. Her legs are bony as hell so I know she's limber than a mufucka. Maybe I shouldn't fuck this up and I'll still be able to spank that shit. I walked over to her and stood directly in front of her. I could feel her hands on me. My massive 6'4" frame towered over her. She stepped up to me and put her tiny titties on my stomach and started grinding her hips with her pussy on my dick. I licked my lips as she turned around and wiggled her ass into me. Just as I started feeling her, my damn two-way went off. I checked the number and saw De's name pop up: MONEY. I stepped back away from her.

"Look I got to roll but I'm a get at you."

"Alright," she said with her back to me.

She picked up her bag slowly and walked to the door switching her ass. I told her to go ahead and leave because I had to get shit together before I skated. When she closed the bedroom door I pulled the brown damage bag from under the bed. I counted the stacks and made sure it was $500,000. I looked through the bag and counted the burners. Yup- four 9mm, five duce-duce caliber pistols, and ten silencer clips. That's what's up. The money De collects from the strip will cover that other change, so we straight. I packed the shit up and went downstairs. It's Kevin and Dennis's shift now. We got two workers rotating three shifts so it was always somebody here. First to keep money constantly flowing, second because there is no way to lock the door from the outside. No hinges on the door and bars on all of the windows to keep mufuckas from running up in here. I waited for the last customer to close the front door before I opened the door to the crib. I looked out the peephole and checked the hallway. I told those niggas to be safe and smart before I rolled out. I walked over to my ride and put the bag in the hide shit away compartment of the Escalade EXT. I jumped in the whip. My two-way went off again as I revved up and pulled off.

Imani

I lay in my bed listening to the wake of a storm. I let my eyes close as Avant's smooth voice poured through my speakers. I traced the silhouette of my shoulder with my fingertips sliding down to the voluptuous curves of my 40D breasts. As the melody of *Making Good Love* continued, I caressed my caramel delights making my body feel like silk. I indulged myself with the smoothness of my entity causing my hips to bounce erotically to the rhythm. I felt the swell between my thighs tell me I'm ready to explore tantalizing sex with nature. Rumbles of thunder echoed throughout the sky followed by streaks of lightening. In an instance heavy rain began to fall battering against my window fiercely. The candles on my dresser flickered as if they were telling me the storm was coming inside.

I began to think about the only man who invaded my space with a real desire to share my life. Memories of candle lit bubble baths and moon lit dinners surfaced. I smiled as immediately my thoughts rushed to Terrell. He showed me that love should be tender like a misty rain. Coming softly but flooding a river. Terrell treated me as if I were a precious diamond at a time when devastation became me. Before I met Terrell I foolishly welcomed men into my life with my pussy. Huh. I naively thought that was what big-bodied women had to do. But Terrell told me I was a limited commodity amongst a species of felines. He always said the right thing at the perfect time to make me smile. I remember hand-held walks down Penn's Landing, ferry rides to Jersey, and store front portraits on South Street. I remember drive in movies. Arguments. Guns. Screams. Bullets. Glass shattering around me, people running. I remember Terrell falling and bleeding in my lap. Tires screeching. Sirens coming too late. Terrell dying in my arms. I sat up in my bed solemnly. I bit my bottom lip and held on to my tears as if they are all I have left in the world. I have been haunted by the night Terrell was killed for over two years. I tell myself since I can't control the nightmares I can at least control the tears. Come on Imani, get it together girl.

I stood up and walked over to my vanity. My diamond shaped mocha eyes twinkled in the candlelight; my caramel complexion glowed in the darkness. The structure of my round cheeks and indents of my deep dimples gives my smile a wicked mysterious appeal. My golden streaked hair cascades seductively over my shoulders. The fullness of my hips and thickness of my ass intimidates every woman who isn't sure of herself. Probably because I walk with the elegance and grace of a gazelle. Do my ladies run it, phat asses and flat stomachs? I get it from my momma.

Cierra, my homegirl, tells me I have an esoteric sex appeal. She says my aura is gorgeous, which confuses the average man. She thinks that's why I celebrate the "Down for Whatever Chilling on the Corner Brothers." Cierra is my girl from the cradle to the grave. I remember in tenth grade at Franklin Learning Center high school, when I was the little fat girl with glasses that everyone loved to hate. Until the new girl from Virginia came to Mount Airy. Cierra was my fairy godmother who rescued me and made me Belle of the Ball. Cierra's a free spirit, she's constantly making moves. Being an only child she knows how to manipulate a conversation and make you see things her way. She definitely has to have her way at all times. If you can't get with her program than she's not feeling you, especially the brothers. There have been hundreds lusting after the red-bone temptress from Hampton. Men shower her with gifts like Benzes, beach houses, private jets, condos in St. Croix. But the only people Cierra will go out of her way for, besides me, are her parents. She will do some tricks for mommy and daddy dearest, that's how she ended up at Georgetown. That didn't last too long though. When it finally occurred to her that she was flunking out she tried to get some dude she met at a basketball game for a couple of dollars. When that plan blew up in her face she withdrew from the University and put all of her stuff in storage. That was six years ago. Since then she has established herself as an independent model in Spain, Italy, and Paris. She's in Italy now but she calls everyday no matter what time it is in America.

I walked across my cream plush carpet over to my window seat. I sat down and parted my Venetian blinds searching for the moon through the falling rain and dark passing clouds. I exhaled deeply. My phone rang interrupting my serenity. I got up and caught the phone just before the machine picked up.

"Hello."

"Yes, is this Imani Heaven Best founder, President and CEO of Miracle Media Consultants Incorporated," the voice on the opposite end said.

I laughed.

"Why yes it is, what can I do for you sir?"

I felt his smile through the phone.

"You can blow me some suga Nae Nae. I am very proud of you baby girl."

I sat on my bed and blew a kiss through the receiver.

I smiled, grateful I have a father who nurtures my dreams. After a drunken fool took my mom from us my dad made my brother Amir and I his number one priorities in life. Amir was only seven, but I was thirteen and I understood that the accident stole mommy away and she wasn't coming back. Even though mommy was gone daddy was always home now and he channeled his pain by giving us everything we needed and wanted. My dad manages the two bar-be-que joints he and his brothers own and run together. Before the accident he lived in those stores. He then instilled in me the initiative to strive for my dreams. He told me the sky is the limit for ordinary folks, but I am extraordinary so I can go beyond the sky. That's why he chose Heaven as my second name.

Dad asked if the meeting with the general manager was finalized. I grinned slyly.

"No doubt," I said ecstatically. "You know basketball is my first love."

After months of phone tag with the general manager of the Philadelphia 76ERS, I finally secured a meeting. It's not until after the '01-'02 season, but I knew interning with The Daily News sophomore and junior year would pay off. Network. Network. Network. You can't stop me now. I marveled over what I've accomplished after completing my masters at Temple University, Spelman is my alma mater.

I purchased and successfully renovated a high-rise office in Centre Square in downtown Philly overlooking the Clothespin, which is a major tourist attraction. I designed the reception area with black leather chairs arranged in a semi circle with foot - stools positioned in front of every other chair. Pine wood end tables on either side of the outside chairs are garnished with Romanesque statutes Cierra shipped to me from Italy. Potted tree plants outline every corner and realms of black and tan check-ered carpet cover hard wood floors. Five seven-foot stained glass windows reflect sunlight off of three crystal chandeliers descend-ing from the ceiling. Two sets of double doors etched with ceramic artwork separate the corridor leading to my office. A simple push of a button on a remote opens and closes the door to the conference room in the rear of my office. Inspirational paint-ings from the Harlem Renaissance are hung proudly from every wall in the suite. I placed a red oak serving table in front of the back wall of the reception area where I plan to keep fresh coffee, tea, juice and the usual morning pastries. With the doors to the rest of my life scheduled to open I definitely have to buckle down and maintain. I'm focused man.

"How's the rest of the proposal coming?" Dad asked like the concerned parent he is.

"Yes sir," I said reminiscent of the tone I used as a teenager when dad asked if my chores were done before he let me go out-side.

I'm actually very pleased with the final draft of my proposition extended to the Sixers to adopt my firm as their media-consulting agency. I'm extremely confident in the techniques I outlined to improve the public perception of athletes through media coverage. If all goes according to plan I'll have the Sixers on my team with the rest of the NBA to follow, not to mention other professional leagues. I shivered gleefully with the thought of my dream coming true. Dad and I made small talk about Amir and the bar-be-que joints for the next half hour, then we said good night.

"I love you Nae Nae. Maybe I'll stop by your office tomorrow."

"Okay. The couches for my office were delivered yesterday but my desk and bookcases along with my display case are being delivered tomorrow." I thought for a moment. "I also have seven interviewees tomorrow."

"Well, like I say, take care of business first," he said with his usual chuckle. "We'll do lunch when you're through."

"I love you old man. Good night."

I hung up the phone and placed it on the charger. I pulled back my cranberry and cream comforter and spread. I took off my cream terry cloth robe and threw it on my Versace love seat. I set my alarm clock for seven and got in the bed. I was asleep before my head hit the pillow.

Quinnzell Supreme Sharpe

I pulled up to the Palace at midnight. It's mad people outside geared up, looking fly ready to get their party on. The line outside is thick as hell so I know the crowd already inside is crazy. When De and me opened this spot two years ago I never thought we would get this many props. Shit, every night we got a capacity crowd. It's funny to me because we only needed the spot to front the dough we were collecting on the streets. I told De we needed a business to keep our funds legitimate. De got the idea to open up a club because he was always throwing hotel parties every weekend anyway. So we coped this spot on 52nd & Parkside and hooked it up.

Once you give your keys to the valet and get past our beefed up security, you'll find yourself on a red carpet surrounded by dim red lights. A few burgundy leather chairs and couches line either side of the carpet, with chill rooms on both sides. Continuing down the aisle, the carpet will lead you to a set of sliding glass doors. Beyond the doors the lighting changes from dim red to black lava lamps. The exotic bar and its maids will mesmerize you, for real. A fish tank replaces the wall behind the bar. De keeps that shit stocked with some wild shit. I think he even got a shark in that jawn now. A swing, surrounded by four crystal chandeliers hung in the shape of a baseball diamond, is over the bar. We call the bar area the Portal because from here you can go to one of three phases of the Palace.

To the left is Phase I. Phase I is the Scene, two dance floors with four rotating dj's with crazy mixes and flows all night. Phase II is the Show, two rooms 6 & 9 with male and female shaky butts. Behind the bar is Phase III. Phase III is the Stage. The stage is where all the concerts go down. I parked my ride, grabbed my bag and headed for the basement. The basement is the office where we go to handle shit. MEMBERS ONLY. You can't even get to the basement through the club, but we can get to the club through the basement. De set that shit up like that. We got cameras hooked up all over the club, inside and out. We clock shit on the multi digital TV. screens hooked up to a computer.

I walked around back and saw Dezionne's silver Lexus LX450. She's the only person allowed to park back here except for extreme circumstances. Dezionne is De's wifey and shit. She manages the Palace and she's the one holding shit down basically. I walked down the steps towards the door and rang the bell for Dezionne to come unlock the gate.

"Who the fuck is that?"

I instantly knew that voice.

"It's the Philadelphia Police, we got guns and shit," I said.

Blue Streak is one of De's favorite flicks because Martin got away with the diamond and shit. The big payback, yamean.

"What the deal Preme, Hold up."

I heard the three deadbolt and chains unlock. De pulled the door open so I knew the two bottom locks weren't locked. He unlocked the gate and pushed it open for me. I stepped inside and locked shit back down. I gave De a pound and we headed down the hall to the office. He put his arm around my neck so I knew he had news. I turned to look at him. He was smiling showing his dimples and shit. De is a pretty mufucka. Hazel-green eyes, curly hair, and his Hershey skin is smoother than most females.

"What's cracking dude, why were you blowing my shit up like a little ho?" I said laughing at him.

"You hold the tail and let me fuck the cat," he said opening the door to the office.

That was his way of telling me he would tell me when the time was right. When I saw Dezionne sitting at the bar counting stacks I knew now wasn't the time. Stan was cleaning gats at the table in the corner, watching Belly on the movie screen. Nino and Cash were shooting pool. De took the bag off my shoulder and sat it on the coffee table in front of the couch. I went to get a drink from the bar.

"What's going on Quinn?" Dezionne asked.

She didn't even look up from the loot. Dezionne's bad as shit. Bachelor's degree in Business from Morgan State. Pretty face, def body. She's the quiet type and they are usually the freakiest females. Don't cause no drama but know how to maintain in the heat of battle. I can talk to her about shit and she'll always give her honest opinion. Not to hurt my feelings, but to keep it gangster.

"That female on the swing last night was going on," I said smiling. "She was the bomb, were her eyes really green?"

"Q, you ask me that every time I put a new girl on the swing. I told you it's just the light, macaroni."

Dezionne rotates the swingers every two days so niggas don't get bored looking at the same chick, but she gives them enough to make them want to pay for the girl in a show. She poured my drink, the usual E&J and coke.

"Don't hate on the hot boyz just because you under lock and key, yamean."

"She's not under lock and key, she's under love and commitment chump," De said walking up behind me. "What's up baby?"

He kissed Dezionne, and their initial greeting turned into five minutes of tongue and lips. I picked up my drink and went over to the couch. I picked up the money logs for each of the Phases off of the table and sat down. We track each Phase separately and also keep a collective log with the money from the Portal. Me and Double D, that's what I call DeShawn and Dezionne, are the only ones who handle the Palace business. The team strictly handles the streets. Shit, with the workers getting knocked every other month we got to get our shit together out there. De came over and sat beside me drinking a Corona.

"What we going to do about the niggas on the block?" I asked De.

He sipped his drink.

"You know that nigga Stan think he the cleaner from the Professional." He put his bottle on the table. "I'm a put that nigga on the block with them cats. Any shiesty shit he know what it is."

"They the only ones fucking up. The crib is holding it down on the money side of things."

"Yeah, I checked out the bag, shit is on point," De said as he split a Dutch. "You been inside?"

I knew exactly why he asked that question. We know each other better than we know ourselves. Jovan must be on the swing. Dezionne hooked her up with a gig as a barmaid and she performs anytime a talent scout or label rep is in the house. Her voice, oooohhhhh weeee, as rich and soulful as Billie Holiday. She and Dezionne were roommates at Morgan State but they didn't graduate together. Needless to say Jovan's hot to def, a cinnamon goddess with a diamond cut body.

"Nah big brother. What's cracking tonight?"

"Jovan's creamy booty in a leopard thong," De said. "Are you going to spank that or what?"

She's sweet on me, but I don't play her too close. Jovan has three kids and two baby daddies. With her circumstances she really can't offer me anything besides pussy and I need much more than that. Stan walked up before I could say anything.

"Yo, I'm fixin to make moves to the block," Stan said screwing a silencer on the gat he had in his hands.

"Alright, but don't fuck nobody up. Matter of fact take Nino and Cash with you and page me if shit goes down," De said and lit his chronic up.

"Remember, you watching for cops. Don't post up with the workers," I said sipping my drink. "And tell them niggas to stay of the corners."

One thing about our team is we all have respect for each

other. No jealousy or hate among the brothers. We look out for each other.

"Alright little nigga, I got you. We're out."

I got up to lock the door behind those niggas. Dezionne left too, to go peep the scene inside. She doesn't like using the passage that leads to the VIP section of the Stage. I walked back over to the couch, picked up my drink and tossed it back. De smiled up at me blowing smoke from his nostrils.

"Dig this Fam," he said passing me a Corona. "My baby is fitting to have my baby."

Damn, that shit caught me off guard. My mind raced back to senior year. This female I fucked after a game told me she was knocked up with my seed. She was hollering some shit like kids are for married mufuckas and wanted some change for an abortion. Hell nah I wasn't going to marry the chick, but I damn sure wasn't killing my seed. I told her I would take care of the baby by myself, but she wasn't feeling that. A week later, she withdrew from the University and my seed is out there running around without me. If I had it in me to call a female a bitch, she would be one all day. But constantly witnessing my bastard ass pop viciously attack my moms' with that word fucked me up. He never talked to her. Instead he barked at her slicing her spirits, with every word bruising her as if he struck her with his bare fists. I still see her teary bloodshot eyes mixed with pain, hate, and disgust. Mom always said fighting in Vietnam made him cold like that. I promised myself I would never shatter a female's character like he did. Damn the circumstances of my situation. It was as if De was reading my thoughts.

"Fuck bitches, especially the one we rode in on, for real," he said.

I sat down on the chair beside him and sipped my Corona.

"Money if you happy, you know I'm ecstatic out this mufucka."

"Hell yeah I'm happy. Every thug needs a lady," De said puffing his blunt. "And you know when you found her ass."

Double De met at a step show my sophomore year. Dezionne competed with her sisters of Delta Sigma Theta Sorority Inc who won that year. As soon as De peeped her it was no denying he wanted her. In the beginning, they had a mutual understanding that their relationship was strictly sexual. But as time went on their attraction intensified. Shit, her peoples still don't know she was in Philly every other weekend or that two of her dorm dressers had De's clothes in them.

"See," De said smoking his chronic. "Niggas be kicking that dumb ass shit, as long as I got wifey I can fuck any bitch. Them niggas is confused, it's as long as I got wifey fuck those bitches. Feel me.

"Most of these jawns will give their panties up because you pulled up in some hot shit sitting on twenty-fours. They see a little cash, icy neck and wrists, they on it quick. But a lady ain't impressed by that shit"

"It's two sides to that shit dude," I said sitting my empty Corona bottle on the table. "Sis definitely got to come deeper than that too."

"Oh no question baby boss. She has to complete you so it will be no need for you to press no other bitch for shit. You and wifey got to be like brothers on some real shit."

"De Money Bags bout to have a little shorty," I said wrapping him up in a headlock. "The block ain't ready."

We laughed for the next three minutes. Damn, I admired my brother.

Imani

"A little to the left," I said to the musty deliveryman who after assembling my display case, desk, and bookcases insisted upon hanging my oil painting of Malcolm X and Dr. King.

"I got it sweet thing," he said turning towards me with his tongue hanging from his mouth.

I know where this was going. Like Chris Rock said anytime a man is being nice all he's doing is offering dick.

"You know, I really appreciate all of your help but really I can handle this," I said as professionally as possible.

Chris Rock also said a woman knows if she's going to fuck a man within the first five minutes of meeting him. And Mr. Delivery Man didn't make the cut. He did do a great job with my furniture. Especially the desk. Its brilliant brass legs and trimmings reflect the smooth texture of the cherry-pine wood. The curved shaved edges give its structure the perfect semi-circle form. Shit, it was amazing that he hung the picture perfectly when his eyes never left my thighs. I was relieved when his partner came back with my credit card and receipt. I thanked them, showed them both out, and locked the door to my suite. I walked back through the reception area to my office and was in awe, but now is not the time for antics. I sat down in my leather lounger and picked up the folder with my interviewees resumes from my desk when the phone rang.

"Good morning and thank you for calling Miracle Media," I said in my usual pleasant tone. "This is Imani H. Best, how may I assist you?"

"Why is the founder of a soon to be prestigious corporation

answering the phone."

I smiled recognizing Cierra's voice as soon as she spoke.

"What's going on long distance Diva?"

"Everything as usual, but you still haven't answered my question sugar."

"Well, my first assistant interviewee should be here in about an hour baby doll," I said. "I'm reviewing resumes as we speak."

"Good. Sweetie I called to tell you that I should have a break in my schedule in a couple of months."

"That's what's up." I haven't seen Cierra in over six months. With her juggling fashion shows, photo shoots, commercials, and movies I know my girl needs a break. "We can relax and get our party on."

"No doubt. I got to run sugar, I have a photo shoot in about twenty minutes. I'll call you tonight. Love you bunches."

"Love you too girl, you better work it."

I spent the remainder of the morning and early afternoon organizing my office. Pausing briefly to interview six stale women who are obviously painfully bitter about their life choices. I mean which direction are some of my beloved sisters headed? Handfuls of us lack ambition and are starving for a hint of pride and firmness of mind. Some are lost and don't want to stand on their own feet because they're too busy waiting for welfare and child support checks.

I shook my head and picked up a picture of me and mom from the box on the floor labeled memoirs. I slid my fingers across the cool glass covering our images trapped in time and space. Not wishing to go back there, only wanting her here now. Lila Sianni Ingle-Best was one of the most phenomenal women ever to grace this earth. I will damn sure follow in her gracious footsteps by up-holding her legacy of success. I feel her pride beaming on me as she watches me fill the right side of my display case with my degrees, honorary plaques, and notoriety awards. And to my left with framed newspaper articles, trophies and photos of gratitude for participating in any and all public service venues where I was able to lend a hand.

I emptied the last box and collapsed on the couch. I kicked off my brown-suede Prada shoes as my body sank into the soft leather. I breathed a deep sigh and hoped my final applicant would at least be hooked on phonics, but I can't speculate. I smiled to myself and thought about how I need to master my video for campaign endorsements and start the power point presentation. Instead I decided to hit Derek up just to pass time, but as soon as I sent the two-way, I wish I hadn't.

I met Derek a few weeks ago when I began moving into my suite after renovations were complete. I accepted his theater tickets and dinner reservation even though Cierra told me it was against my good graces. He's a tall, sexy-fine African African-American Studies professor at University of Pennsylvania who takes his profession extremely literal. As a former Black Panther and current NAACP activist, he allows his work to consume his every thought. Believe me, I too recognize and support my peoples constant on-going struggle for equal rights and opportunities. And don't get me wrong Derek makes valid and substantial points about injustice, poverty, and discrimination but the blame is no longer solely on 'the man'. He may be the one giving us the drugs and guns, but we are the ones killing ourselves with it. Though they are the ones who construct the warheads, bombs, and nuclear weapons that kill all of us. They got money for wars but can't feed the poor. We can't win for losing. When I heard Derek's tone on the phone I knew he was about to start ramming.

"Imani, I just saw Capital One's jungle boogie commercial," he said.

His irate tone boomed through the receiver. Damn, I can't even get upset because I already know his steelo and I paged him anyway. So like always, I owned up and took responsibility for my actions. I put the phone on speaker and lay back on the couch for the duration.

"They're calling us monkeys subliminally because whitey is intimidated by strong black warriors in reality. See, that's why they gave Denzel an academy award for Training Day and not Malcolm X. In Malcolm X, crackers were displayed in their reality form where as Training Day showed them subliminally. Same for Halle. What about Losing Isaiah, Queen, or Introduction to Dorothy Dandridge? No. She gets an academy award for being naked in Monsters Ball. And not to hate on Denzel and Halle, but Morgan Freeman Angela Basset, Danny Glover, Whoopi, and Samuel L. played in more vital roles: A Time to Kill, The Color Purple. But crackers say fuck us because they set the standard of quality for the Grammy's, Guild, Emmys and Academy Awards."

I was relived when the bell to my suite rang. I hung up with Derek and headed to the door. I told him I would think about accepting his dinner invitation. Funny how he managed to slide that in. I wouldn't mind going out with Derek but he has to chill with the lectures.

I cleared my mind of all lingering negativity still brewing from my earlier applicants and opened the door for Jovan Hunter. She walked in wearing a fierce ice blue Donna Karen pant suit with diamond buttons lining the front of her waist length blazer. Her navy and ice blue checkered shoes match her pocketbook and neck scarf exactly. Her shinny black hair is pulled up in a neat bun accented by sliver chopsticks, which accentuated her brown sugar eyes. After reviewing her resume, I definitely thought Jovan was dressed for her success. I led her to the conference room.

"Ms. Best, I would like to thank you for giving me this opportunity."

"Please call me Imani."

She smiled.

"Imani."

"Have a seat. I see you went to Morgan State. I love to see more of us are choosing Historically Black Colleges and Universities."

"Definitely. Our schools are extremely underrated. Except on BET."

"This should be shamefully credited to the mayor's office and the school board. The poor quality in the public school system and constant budget cuts redundantly proves keeping our children's education inferior is on someone's to do list. I apologize I've moved from the subject. Tell me Jovan what is your greatest attribute?"

"Imani you are very profound. And to answer your question, my wit. It keeps the opposition on its toes and closes deals swiftly."

"Eye on the prize."

"Exactly."

"What would you say hinders you the most professionally?"

"Taking on too many projects at one time."

"Same script, different cast."

"I guess we're two of a kind."

"And that's a recipe for prosperity. I'll see you Monday."

I shook Jovan's hand and walked her out front. I locked up my suite and headed to my car elated I'd found my perfect compliment. I have a feeling she'll work as hard as I do, which says a lot about her in my eyes. I pulled up to O'Hara's and parked my Bentley behind a black Bonneville. Dad was standing in front of the restaurant waiting for me. I joined him and we went in together.

Quinnzell Supreme Sharpe

I rolled after we bust a grub at IHOP. Jovan asked me to come chill with her even though she told Dezionne she had to get up early. And with the morning sun rising on her face I knew what it was and it's nothing. De went to Dezionne's crib up in Germantown so I have the crib to myself. De and I got a hot spot out in Mt. Laurel, New Jersey. Something De learned a long time ago, don't do business near or where you rest your head. Since we're planning to lock Philly down completely on the cream side of things, quiet town New Jersey is the obvious get-a-way chill spot.

Nobody knows where we stay. Nobody. Of course Dezionne be at the crib but she comes by car always in a blindfold and she understands why. It's about protection from the reality of our hustle. Streets will do anything to your Queen to burn you. So the less she knows the better, yamean. Dezionne respects the game and trusts De enough to know it ain't about no other females or some shiesty shit. Like De said, every thug needs a lady. A ride or die, Bonnie and Clyde type, chick who can piece shit together. The team, we keep it neutral. We have a big ass office at the Palace and a few DL spots to handle BI. Matter fact they're "L" spots, even lower than "DL," yamean. We don't hold any personals, business has always been business.

I pulled up to the crib and parked the Escalade in the eight-car garage with the rest of the wheels and chilled in the gazebo. I took off my Timbs and laid back on the swing. I usually chill out here to get my mind right after shit goes down. Sometimes I sit sideways on the hammock, or light candles around the hot tub and chill in there. But the twinning vines of peach and ivory lilies surrounding fences of the gazebo have basically been my ears. They pedal perspective yamean. The breeze rocked me to sleep 'til around one 'o clock. I picked up my boots and went in the crib. I had six messages on my two-way. Tiana, Candi, Kelley, Tionne, Jovan, and Shakera. Damn. If females are supposed to be so different, why are they all kicking the same shit but ain't saying anything. I skipped steps going up the carpeted spiral staircase to the bathroom. I turned on my Art of Noise CD Moments in Love is my shit, it's all pulse. Niggas be trying to clown my slow jams and shit. I just tell them, yo, you can't romance a female with Jay-Z. Shit, I rocks Jigga all day but ain't nobody freaking to H to the IZO.

I sat in the shower seat and let the steaming water massage my body. Droplets of water soaked my head and face then cascaded down my neck to my chest. I got up and stood in the center of the drenching six headed circular showerhead. Since I ain't take my morning piss yet my dick is so hard, Mr. Miyagi couldn't chop that shit with a karate chop. Not that he would get a chance to. I could go let one of those jawns kiss him real quick but we got a lunch meeting at O'Hara's in a minute. I washed my ass, threw on some fresh RocaWear, jumped in the Boni and rolled out. De was waiting at our usual corner table where we peep everybody who rolls through the door.

"What's up Money?" I said walking over to the table. De stood up to give me a pound.

"You, super Supreme, getting crème, making the ladies feen."

"Hah. Whatever nigga," I said. "You order my drink?" We sat down and De nodded towards my glass.

"That's what's up," I said. "Yo, what's up with going to the game on Sunday?"

I gulped down my E&J and picked up a Corona.

"Cool. Damn, that's right baby," De said damn near drooling. "If the thighs ain't touching the pussy can't marinade."

I looked up to see the woman who had the power to make my

whole body glow. Fuck the Last Dragon. Baby didn't even need theme music to make the crazy rhythm in her hips. She moved confidently through the room as if she possessed a sacred treasure and knew no one could touch her. Her brown suede pants groped her onion ass, hugged her sexy thighs, and flared over her tight calves. She's thick, heavy booty, vicious curves in all the right places. You can see that thing from the front, it's lethal. Beautiful face. Gorgeous, I'm a say mocha eyes. Sis is bad as shit. There's something about her I definitely have to get at. De must have seen the look in my eyes.

"Damn Preme. I never saw you peep a female this hard dude."

He's right. She got my full attention without saying one word. I couldn't take my eyes off of her.

"Yo, I got to holla at her."

She's with this old head dude who looks like he could be her pops.

"Shit," De said when Nino and Cash walked in without Stan. The look on their faces told us something went down.

"Yo call Dr. Quick niggas," Cash said lighting a cigarette.

De hooked up with Dr. Quick a couple of years ago. We had to show some out of town niggas what time it was and our war wounds don't get hospitalized.

"Explain on the way," De said getting up from his seat.

I got up and De whispered to me as we walked out if she's the one meant for you, you'll see her again, trust. We walked outside. Nino hopped in Dezionne's wheel with De and headed to the spot with Cash following. I walked over to my ride. A drop-top Cranberry Bentley, mirror tinted out, sitting on 22's was behind the Boni. For some reason I know it's hers. Big time females attract hood –rich big ballas. Ain't got no job, but I stay sharp. I got in the whip and headed down Chestnut Street to the Palace. I came down the Mann Music Center curve and drove past the club to the Mobil on 52nd & Lancaster. I got six strips and a biscuit, and a three-piece dark for De, from Crown Fried

Chicken and shot back down to the club. I pulled up to the Palace at the same time as Cash. We parked and walked around back to the office. De and Nino were sitting at the round table waiting on us. I put De's food down in front of him.

"Good looking out yo," he said. "I'm hungrier than a run-a-way slave."

"It's cool nigga, you know we cooler than three breezes."

"Oh, but you don't give a fuck if I eat or not Supreme," Nino said.

"You sound like a little ho," I said laughing. "Shit nigga, y'all the reason why we're here and not at O'Hara's sitting behind a big ass plate of crab legs."

"Yo, Blaze is on his way to grip that nut ass nigga up, and he going to take him to the ducky spot on Paschall," Cash said hanging up the phone. "Dr. Quick said that nigga Stan need ten stitches to close his chest up, but he cool."

"Blaze going to fuck dude up," Nino said splitting a Dutch.

That nigga Blaze is just like O 'Dog from Menace II Society: young, black, and don't give a fuck. America's worst nightmare. Only life ain't a movie. Blaze is a straight up hit- man and any nigga who cross the crew is a ghost. Nino broke down what happened while De and I ate.

"This dude walked up on the set talking big shit," Nino said lighting the chronic up. "Dude was causing a scene talking about y'all bitch ass niggas getting too much cream on the block and shit and he ain't eating enough.

Nino passed the blunt to Cash.

"Stan got out of the car to go dead that shit, dude turned around with a blade. He sliced that nigga and boned out. We chased him but he was fast as shit and we ain't catching no crackheads. Pookie and Mann jumped in the wheel but 5-0 was cruising. We paged y'all niggas and got no response."

"Yeah but like I said I know where he be pumping at," Cash said smoking. "Right up there on 60th & Chestnut. My young freak stays on Samson Street and shit."

"If dude hustle out west why the fuck is he clocking our dollars," I said.

Cash passed the blunt to De, but he didn't take it. He had his game face on. I know he's piecing shit together on the mentals. My two-way went off and Jovan's number popped up. Damn, she got it bad.

"What's up niggas," I said putting my two-way back in my pocket.

"How the fuck we suppose to know nigga," Nino said.

"We're going to find out," De said getting up. "Interrogation before assassination. We out."

Imani

After an hour and a half of finger licking and laughter I said good night to my Dad. I walked outside to my car and saw a damn ticket on my windshield. Way to end a bomb ass day. I took the paper off of the windshield to read it.

Yesterday is history
Tomorrow a mystery
Today is a gift
That's why it's called the present

Quinnzel

Quinnzel, huh. Get the fuck out of here. I balled that shit up and threw it away. I got in my car and rolled. I pulled up to Walnut Lane Terrace around six. I parked in my spot and went upstairs to my apartment. I opened the door and was greeted by the sweet aroma of the black love incense I burned this morning. I took off my shoes, put my briefcase on the floor, and hit play on my answering machine. I hit the erase button as soon as I heard Troy's voice. I ain't a salad; he's not tossing me twice. I waited two months too long for him to check his Baby Mama, because I don't want to hurt the bitch. She plays on my phone, saw me in King of Prussia Mall and her and her tack head homies called themselves following me. I told Troy to put her in check before I checked her damn chin. Obviously he can't handle her because I'm still getting late night hang-ups. So I decided he was guilty by association and cut his ass off. Every once in a while he'll call me, still trying to taste my taffy. That's funny to me. Derek's message played next telling me he'd be here at eight. He called right before I left the office. I was so hype about my new employee, Jovan, when he asked me if I made my mind up about dinner I just said yes. Besides, I want the presence of a man tonight.

My feet sank into my white carpet as I walked across the living room to my entertainment center. I turned on my surround sound system and Teena Marie's sultry voice poured through my six feet tall speakers. I sat the remote on the coffee table and went in the kitchen. I poured a glass of Hennessey mixed with Red Passion Alize and went out on the balcony. I leaned on my railing and the cool passing breeze molested my naked toes. I twirled the ice in my glass and sipped my thug passion mix. Terrell drunk thug passion every day. I looked up at the hazy sky and wondered if I would ever again have sincere love like his. I feel sadness and tears coming on. Damn. I went inside. I sat my empty glass on the kitchen counter and went in the bathroom. I pulled back my lacy white shower curtain and ran my bath water. I eased my body into the steaming water. The scent of white diamond bath beads tickled my nose. I relaxed my muscles and let the warm water soothe me. I closed my eyes for what I thought was a minute. It was much longer because when I opened them the water was luke warm and my bubble blanket had evaporated.

I wrapped my terry-cloth robe around me and went in my bedroom. I turned the light to its first setting and sat on my bed. I oiled my body and sprayed Jovan White Musk on my sensual places. I slipped on my hip hugging spaghetti strapped Versace dress and matching sandals. I pulled my hair up and styled it in a bun. I put diamond studs in all four of my ear holes, and closed the clasps on the matching tennis bracelet and watch. My CD player shuffled and played Paula Abdul's old school jam, Rush-Rush. Hurry, hurry love and come to me. My intercom buzzer rang. I picked up my black Coach bag off the dresser and headed for the front door.

"Who is it?"

"Yo, what's up peoples?"

"You ain't gangster nigga."

"Just open the door, for I see why you can't."

I buzzed the door for Amir and sat my bag on the table. Amir came in dipped out as usual. My little brother stays fly as shit. And he doing his thing at MIT, you can't tell him shit. But you know I got to fuck with him.

"You think you housing shit young one."

"My game stays tight," Amir said. He kissed my cheek. "I'm so hot, I make disease sick."

"Doggy, you still eating cookies with the rookies while I'm drinking coffee and eating doughnuts with the grown ups."

"You got jokes."

I laughed with my brother and sat on the couch. Amir skipped the CD and the Clipse's LP Lord Willin' came on.

"What you know about the Clipse."

"You playing it ain't you."

"Let me find out Nae is thugged out," Amir said nodding his head. "You want a nigga with some Timb boots, don't you?"

"As long as he can lay the pipe."

"I knew you were a freak."

Amir went in the kitchen.

"Yo, Nae where the grub at?"

"I'm about to go out to eat"

"Word, that's cool. I'll order some shit."

"Oh, are you chilling?"

"You know it," Amir said. He opened the drawer and looked through the menus. "Why, where are you going?"

"Out with Derek."

"That nut ass nigga. Damn Nae, get your weight up."

"Now you got jokes."

"Dude is a fucking poindexter."

"Like the smuts you fuck be decent. And you better stop giving those chickens my phone number too."

"Man, they be dickmatized. I be fucking them girls and not

even kissing them."

"You better watch yourself."

"I got it Nae." He grinned at me.

"Whatever."

I fixed another drink and went in my room. The phone rang and stopped.

"Amir, did you get that?"

"Nah nigga, it stopped."

I'm sick of this petty ass bitch. The phone rang again and I grabbed it.

"WHAT!!!"

"Damn, diva all thugged out. What's up?"

"What up C double? This trick keep playing on my phone and shit," I said shaking my head.

"Who, Troy's baby mom?"

"Yeah, I don't know why baby moms think they're invincible and shit."

"I got news," Ciarra anounced. I got a lead role in a new day-time drama."

"Word! You go girl. Do the damn thing."

"You know, you know. But I'm going to have to postpone my trip," Cierra explained.

"It's cool do your thing. What's the pilot like?"

"They're delivering the script next week. And I did peep a lot of fine ass men at the readings. I'm about to get my groove back."

"Like you ever lost it."

Cierra laughed.

"You're the one losing your touch, you better be getting your freak on. You got all those athletes as clients."

"I don't mix business with pleasure." I glanced at myself in the vanity.

"That's why your pussy is shriveling up now, talking that dumb shit. You better holla at AI's little fine ass."

"Hello! He's married. And I'm thorough bred, I can't be that other woman."

"I know that's right," Cierra said. "But Imani, dick is not a deposition. Your workaholic ass needs some flavor."

"I'm married to the firm boo, you gots to understand."

I laughed, Cierra didn't.

"Imani, I'm serious girl. You already know the promise a real man brings and I know you miss it. Your sexy ass is a balla caller so stop playing"

Cierra's renditions always tell me she gives a damn.

"It's not like I don't want a man. But, men need to be needed."

"Don't beat me in the head with the insecure brother bullshit Imani because the men you intimidate won't even approach you. What's really going on?"

I didn't say anything.

"It's Terrell, isn't it?"

I still didn't say anything.

"Imani listen. No one will ever replace Terrell in your heart. But sweetie, you have to let love in. It's another man out there made just for you. And while you're bullshitting with yourself real love could be passing you by."

"I needed to hear that come from someone other than the mirror."

"You know I got your back."

Amir picked up the phone.

"My bad Nae, I'm trying to order this food right quick."

"Amir."

"Yo, who that?"

"Who do you want it to be?"

"Damn what's up Cierra, when can I be your baby daddy?"

"Let's do this." She loved to fuck with Amir.

"Oh, it's like that."

"Yes because I hear you killing them at MIT. Do that baby."

"You know I always got the heat, it's nothing big. So I can freak you, right?"

"Graduate brother," Cierra said laughing.

"Come on now, I mack plenty bitches. I'm trying to make your day."

"Holla back youngin."

"Holla front, Tyra Stanks."

Amir hung up before Cierra could say anything.

"Yo Amir can get it."

"You cannot hump my little brother."

"Damn," Cierra said laughing. "Well, let me let you go sweetie."

"Thank you Cierra."

"Girl please. If I don't hold you down who will?"

"Where would I be without you dog?"

"By your muthafuking self. Bye."

"Peace."

I hung up the phone and went in the living room. As soon as I went out on the balcony, I heard the intercom buzz.

"Nae tight ass is here," Amir said.

I went inside and picked up my bag.

"Why don't you go fall in some pussy because you know the gutted jawns you fuck ain't got no walls. Holla."

I closed the door before Amir could come back. I hopped in Derek's Nisaan 300 ZX and he cranked up the Coltrane. Lowering the volume only to debate with me about stereotypes.

"Imani open your pretty brown eyes sweetheart," he said. "There are no black dramas on any national network. The Cosby Show and A Different World were our only livelihoods. DL Hughley's show was number one when they forced him off. Now if we aren't talking about yo' mama, yo' weave, boyz in da hood killing each other on the corner with their pants eight sizes to big, or backing that thing up there is no longevity. And I despise the fact that they say Venus and Serena only win because of their strength like their skill level and mastery of the game has nothing to do with them winning championship match after championship match."

That dissertation was enough for me to shut what we call the fuck up. But when we got to Capital Grille Derek pitched a bitch because I wanted chicken fingers.

"Imani you can not be serious."

"Excuse the fuck out of me for not having politically correct taste buds. But stewed Bugs Bunny and sautéed Daffy Duck does not sound appealing."

"Rabbit and Duck are acquired tastes."

"Word. I did hear rabbit tastes like chicken. Can they deep fry it and serve it up with some honey mustard?"

"Imani…"

You know what, fuck this.

"I want to go."

"Maybe I can suggest something else."

"No. I want to go now."

I got up and walked to the door. Derek followed like a good little lap dog.

The ride back to my house was silent, for once. Derek pulled up to the door of my building and turned his car off.

"Imani, I do apologize for this evening."

"Great."

Derek leaned over to kiss me. His kiss was wet and sloppy and he damn near swallowed my face. I jumped out of the car and flew up the steps into my building. Remind me never to call him again. I hit myself in the forehead.

Quinnzell Supreme Sharpe

We jumped in the Navigator with Cash to go meet Blaze at the spot. We use the jeeps strictly for BI, so all other wheels stay incognito. Or as I say incognegro. When we pulled up to the back Blaze was pulling dude out of the trunk. He must have made dude strip because he ain't have shit on but his boxers. Blaze is skilled, he moves quickly like a trained assassin. He put dude in the basement and we all went inside. Dude was lying on his stomach with his wrists tied behind his back.

"Turn your bitch ass over," Blaze demanded.

Dude struggled to turn his body over but he wound up on his side. Blaze kicked him in his chest and he fell over on his back. Both of his kneecaps were shot. I looked at Blaze. I knew what it was when I met him, yamean. He's like a dog he don't speak but he understands. We hit him up, he handle his hit, get paid, and disappear. We definitely need this nigga on pay roll because I ain't a killer. I can't have that shit on my heart. I'll fuck a nigga up on sight and if I have to I'll handle myself, but I'm not about no murder one shit.

"Since your plug ass don't do shit but hug the block," De said lighting a cigarette. "Who do you hustle for?"

Dude ain't say shit.

"Oh you can't holla," Blaze said. He drug a canister of gasoline over from the cabinet. "Blaze'll make you scream."

He unscrewed the cap and poured the bottle of death all over dude. Sure enough he started screaming.

"It's a fucking miracle," Blaze said backing up.

"I'm a ask you just one more time before my man light you

the fuck up with some hot shit," De said. He puffed his cigarette and blew a ring of smoke from his mouth.

"Big Time. Big Time," dude said crying.

"Do you peoples," I said walking towards the door. "Let's roll my niggas, we got the info we came for."

Blaze is going to take dude to the train tracks and set him on fire. I don't need to see that shit. He knows where to pick up the rest of his loot. We rolled back to the Palace.

De went to give Dezionne her wheels and pick up his. I told him I would meet him at the club later and went to the crib. I got to the crib around five-thirty. I went in the game room and fell back on the plush love seat. I turned on the PS2 that's hooked up to the digital surround sound movie screen. Our shit be rocking NBA Live 3000. But since this 2K2 shit is kicking my ass, I turned it off and went upstairs. Oh shit, Gargoyles is on. I laid back on my king sized canopy bed and put my head on the cushioned headboard. My reflection bounced from the head board mirror to my floor model TV screen. Gargoyles are the truth even though it's a cartoon. Their theme is the code I live by. A gargoyle can no more stop protecting his castle then breathing the air. Only I'm not a gargoyle I'm a warrior and my castle is my family. Fuck those cars, this house. I straight ride or die for my miz, Double D, and my wife and children when they come to me. I thought about my seed living without knowing me. It fucks me up everyday because even if the jawn wanted to look for me, she couldn't. Dames who don't have my last name only know me as Supreme, and I honestly don't remember her name either. I called my miz to check in on her. She wasn't at the crib so I left her a message. Me and De bought her a beachfront condo in L.A. Even though I hate the Lakers with a passion. I took it down 'til ten o'clock. I must have been tired as shit. I took a shower and threw on my fuck the night up gear. Brown Kangol. Stacey Adams shoes. Everything I wore, top notch.

I jumped in the silver Lamborghini and rolled to the Palace. I was digging on some big booty chick on the dance floor. Double

De was sexing each other up behind me. DJ Master mixed the reggae flows. The floor is packed than a muthfuka. This chick is rubbing me, throwing her ass into me and I'm not even feeling her. I thought about the woman I would surrender my all to. I'm still tripping over the note, I left on her windshield. I even left my name and shit. Quinnzel. What the fuck, is Supreme actually feeling like this? Since I was fourteen I kept twenty freaks on deck. Not one of them put a move on my heart like she did. I see her angel eyes every time I close mine. De tapped my shoulder and nodded his head towards Jovan.

She prowled her way through the crowd in a black Gucci full-length leather. Toes painted, back all out, ass standing at attention. Damn. I don't know why I'm not feeling this female. As fly as she is, she don't do shit that burns my britches. Jovan freak danced her way into me. Cutie with the booty didn't stand a chance. Jovan moved like a cat in heat, grinding her ass into my dick and shit. She's pumping hard as shit too. DJ Flow mixed in some Soca. The crowd didn't miss a beat, but this is not what I rock. I peeled Jovan off of me and went out to the Portal. Linda Lust is on the swing killing brothers with one look at her triple E titties. She clocks stupid loot in a show. I went over to the bar. Tammy must've seen me coming because my drink was waiting when I walked up. I looked at the entrance to the Stage. It's butter how we ain't have a concert in two months and money is larger than ever. Jovan walked up and wrapped her arms around my waist. I knew it was her because she's the only broad who thinks she got it like that. And she really don't. Jovan is forbidden chocolate.

"Supreme," she whispered in my ear. Her white diamond perfume is bittersweet. "I got a job downtown with Miracle Media Consultants Incorporated."

I don't give a fuck, but I can't kill her in front of millions.

"Oh yeah, what's that?" Jovan slid her sleek, hot body against me as she turned around to face me.

"This sister named Imani founded it," she said sliding her airbrushed press-ons up and down my silk shirt. "I'm an executive administrative assistant but she said I would have to do a lot of hands on stuff like going to pre & post game conferences."

"Game Conferences," I said brushing her hand off of me. She sucked her teeth.

"Yeah, she's all into sports," she said licking my ear. "Why don't you come celebrate with me?"

Shit, a female digging sports. I need to meet her. But this freak in heat gots to go. I stepped away from Jovan and left her standing there. I went and told De I was rolling out; Jovan done fucked my mood up.

Imani

My alarm clock jarred me out of my sleep at six-twenty. I lie awake in my bed craving crazy love making in the morning's rising, complete with breakfast in bed. That sounds like the bomb to me. But since I'm laying here by my damn self I got up and took a shower. I put on my red silk Victoria's Secret dress with the wide legs. The cris-cross tethers on my back matched the straps on my Hugo Boss sandals. I pulled my hair up into a high pony-tail and let my spiral curls dangle on my neck and back. I picked up my red Coach bag, keys, and rolled out.

I spent the day training Jovan, molding her into the perfect executive assistant. Bold, persistent, and forceful, those are necessities without question. Make your presence felt, don't take no for an answer, and don't take no shit. Jovan understood the imperative factors of dominating my craft and above all else attacking the goal. I'm in the business of flourishing via achievement. I take no shorts and thrive at whatever I put my hand to. Try to anyway. And after I heard Jovan humming, I felt some type of way about her not wanting to peruse her talents in the industry. I say, if you are fortunate enough to be blessed with a gift flaunt it in the best way. But to each is own. Jovan gave me a VIP card to the Palace, a club she performs in. I told her I'd come through tonight just for support, I heard the Palace is the bomb.

Later that night, I drove past the massive crowd wrapped around the main entrance of the Palace to VIP. I stepped out of my Bentley rocking four inch silver stilettos. The crystalline jewels on my sandals popped with my silver waist length jacket. Enticing caramel flesh, from my thigh to my ankle, peeks through spiral rings sheared on both sides of my ass gripping leather Gucci pants. I gave my keys to the mesmerized valet, who drooled, all over my ticket. The wind blew through my extra long shear bell-bottom sleeves as I walked to the VIP entrance. I stepped inside the door and walked into a fantasy. The vestibule lit by ten wall mounted lava lamps enchanted the waterfall archway sealed inside of a crystal shell. The waterfalls rushed into glass dolphins perched inside marble pools with cobblestone floor. Okay, VIP. I walked under the archway and followed the red matting to a set of sliding glass doors. I realized the doors were sound proof when they opened and hundreds of voices surrounded me. The doors closed behind me and I was swallowed by a sea of people. I eased my way through the crowd and walked down a glass spiral staircase to the bar. Damn, they have a shark in the fish tank. The Palace is high tech. I sat on a barstool and ordered a Hennessey & Alize. In the dark lighting I saw a shadow floating above me. I looked up to see a vanilla ass swinging from the ceiling.

"What the fuck," I said to myself but loud enough to get the barmaids attention. She's damn near naked too in a bikini and sarong like she's on a beach some damn where. She looked at me and rolled her eyes. I was wondering why so many brothers where just chilling in the center floor. This is not for me. I picked up my drink and walked back through the crowd.

"Damn Sis, can I bite that."

I turned around to see a greasy muscle shirt with gold teeth standing in front of me.

"Hell no, you'll fuck around and bite off my clitoris," I said squinting my eyes to block his shinning grill. I shook my head and kept walking. Was I supposed to be impressed, I don't think so. Anyway, I flowed with the crowd. Automatic doors slid open and Nelly's blazer, "Hot in Here" boomed through a hundred speakers. I danced into the crowd peeping the brothers. Suits, Timbs, bling-bling, white tee shirts, bucket hats, braids, and of course a jerry curl. It's never white tee shirts; I'll try braids for three hundred.

My heart skipped three-four beats when I saw him. Everything and everyone disappeared. My eyes outlined each and every inch of his masterfully chiseled frame. I studied and memorized his beautiful face and meringue mahogany skin. I completely lost myself with one look into his midnight eyes. My heart fluttered when he smiled revealing sexy dimples imprinted in his cheeks. Them shits are epic. He doesn't have braids, but his wavy dark hair is freshly cut. He must have Indian in his family. Edges neat, side burns smooth, mustache and goatee trimmed. I bear witness to his physique of steel. You could slice bread on the shitty sharp creases in his tan Polo khakis. And his cinnamon brown timbs had no scuffs, no scars. He looked in my direction and our eyes danced in a moment of eternity. His eyes never left mine as he came to me. I started shitting bricks as he got closer. He stood right in front of me.

"Excuse me."

The sweet scent of his cologne sent tingles all over my body. His baritone voice echoed in my head and sent chills through my bones. His juicy lips looked so velvety, I wanted to bite them.

"Yes." That is the only word I remember. Whatever he says, that's my answer.

He smiled boyishly and I started melting. I never lose control like this. I don't know what's come over me.

"My name is Quinnzel," he said in my ear.

"Quinnzel." I thought for a minute. "You're the ghost writer."

He smiled flaunting those alluring dimples. Quinnzel took my right hand in his and led me off the floor to a side room in a corner by the main entrance. He sat beside me on a black love seat facing an ocean front sun set trapped inside of a frame. I can actually hear waves crashing. I'm feeling the ambiance. Quinnzel kept his eyes on me. His lasting gaze enticed my imagination.

"How did you know that was my car," I said trying not to sound too shook. But I have to make sure he's not crazy, deranged.

His eyes read my soul.

"Fate." The seriousness in his tone demolished the sheltering barricade I built around this heart of mine.

"What's your name Queen," he said in a softer, reassuring tone.

"Imani H. Best." Shit, I sound so corporate. Why didn't I just give him a business card?

"H." He raised his right eyebrow. Damn, he's gorgeous.

"Heaven."

"Amen." We laughed together.

The clock struck midnight with Quinnzel and I deep in our twelfth conversation. He graduated from Georgetown, he was a b-baller but it wasn't written in the stars for him to continue in that path. He owns this club with his brother DeShawn, who respectably helped bring Quinnzel up and most importantly; he's a Sixer fan. Our flow was wrecked by a knock at the door. Damn, who is disturbing this groove? His expression resembled my thoughts.

"Excuse me."

His b-boy flavor is evident in his stroll. He stepped outside and closed the door behind him. I am definitely feeling Quinnzel. I checked my watch. Oh shit its twelve-thirty. The door opened and my sexual chocolate fantasy appeared.

"Can I get you something," he said sitting down.

"Actually, I have to go." He looked disappointed.

"Will you walk me outside?"

"Most definitely."

We walked out front and I gave my ticket to the valet. People are still filing into the club thick. The driver pulled up with my car and got out. I leaned against the door.

"Good-bye Quinnzel."

He put his finger on my lips and shook his head.

"Don't say good-bye," he said. "Good-bye means forever."

He sounds so sincere. Damn, I want this brother.

"What should I say," I said smiling at him.

He kissed my forehead so gently.

"So long." I was dizzy with euphoria.

"So long Quinnzel." I slipped him my number just before he stepped back on the sidewalk, and I got in my car.

"Good night Imani."

I pulled off, giddy as hell with my thong soggy as shit.

Quinnzell Supreme Sharpe

Once Imani pulled off, I walked around back. De was posted up on Dezionne's wheel rolling a blunt. Fuck is he chilling out here for?

"What's up playboy," I said walking up to him.

"Let's ride nigga." He walked around to the driver side. I got in and we boned out.

"That was your bosom," De said heading down 52nd Street.

I nodded my head.

"Yup, she's the truth like AI."

I peeped her in the club on some enraptured shit. I didn't take my eyes off of her while I stepped to her. We bust it up for a nice young minute. Yamean, an easy conversation. Her mind is definitely right. She runs her own shit, no kids, stands on her own two, and she rides with the Sixers. I pieced two and two together and figured Jovan's ass out to be her assistant. I don't give a fuck though. It ain't shit she can do to fuck this up. De parked on Cobbs Creek and we went and sat in the park. He sparked his blunt up.

"Yo, Jovan works for Imani." I opened the Corona I got from the cooler. De keeps a stocked bar in every ride he push. "It ain't nothing magnetic between me and Jovan, but she spiteful as shit."

"She's a high-class nasty ho," De said puffing his blunt. "But let me ask you a question, where is Imani's head at on the mental?"

I reminisced about our first encounter. Her voice, her smile. Damn, she got me like that.

"She got knowledge of self, book smarts, common sense,

she's stacked."

"Alright nigga calm the fuck down you all swollen about the chest and shit," De said laughing at me. "That's what's up though dude, but listen. You're going to have to come at Jovan's neck on some real shit. Set that broad straight because you know she run her mouth and all types of bullshit come tumbling out and you don't need Imani feeding into that shit."

"I feel you dude. I ain't letting Jovan fuck up shit with me and my future wifey."

"Oh shit what the fuck," De said damn near choking. "You're really feeling shorty ain't you nigga?"

De looked at me like a proud father. I looked him in his eyes when I said, "Most definitely."

"It's like butter baby," he said giving me a pound. "On the real Preme, don't fuck this shit up. Imani is the bomb shorty."

He smiled and nodded his head giving me his approval. That's what's up.

"Yo, what's the science on that cat Big Time," I said getting down to business.

De puffed his blunt.

"I got Rahiem pulling that nigga's cards and shit. I'm a holla at him tomorrow morning."

Rahiem is our 5-0 connect. He's been on the force for like sixteen years and at some point started feeling like he was sacrificing too much with little reward. So for a nice piece of change he tells us what we want to know. Like Danny Devito said in The Heist; everybody wants money, that's why it's called money.

"So we get that nigga's resume, then what?"

"The plot thickens muthfucka," De said standing up. "Let's roll."

The after hours crowd was lined up outside of the Palace. We keep the spot open until five in the morning. That way when the other bars and shit close at two, their customers come here and they don't leave. We rolled up in the spot and hit the dance floor for a minute. Dezionne started feeling sick, so De took her home.

I stayed to close shit up and count the paper. I made it to the crib like seven o'clock, tired than a muthfucka. I'm ready to get my nod on, but I called Imani first. She's been on my mind all night.

"Hello." She sounds wide-awake. I don't do the early morning shit too tough.

"Imani."

"Yes."

"This is Quinnzel," I said fumbling over my words. I don't remember feeling like this. "I was thinking about you and I wanted to hear your voice."

"Aren't you a sweetheart?"

I don't want her to think I'm trying to be sweet; I'm keeping it real out this muthfucka.

"Imani, I'm feeling you and I need you to understand that I don't play games." I kicked off my Timbs. "You are the kind of woman I've waited my whole life for and the only way I know how to come is correct."

I say what I mean and mean what I say.

"Honestly Quinnzel, I've been having some wild feelings of my own." She laughed. "I can't believe I just said that to you."

"Why not?"

"I don't usually put myself on Front Street before the first date."

"Well check this out, why don't you come kick it with me at the Sixers game on Sunday."

"I'm feeling that."

"Cool." I fell back on my bed. "Imani?"

"Yes."

"Thank you."

"For what?"

"For coming into my life." I heard her gasp. "So long beautiful."

"So long Quinnzel."

I hung up the phone and closed my eyes. I pictured Imani standing in her living room smiling her ass off. I went to sleep with visions of Imani's shimmering eyes and vibrant smile. My singing two-way woke me up at twelve-thirty. I don't recognize the number so I used the business line, hooked up in the computer room, to call it back. The name is unlisted so the number comes up unavailable on most caller ids.

"Good Afternoon and thank you for calling Miracle Media Incorporated."

Shit, from the tone of Jovan's voice I thought I called the fucking phone sex hotline. Now is as good a time as any to kick the ballistics with her.

"Yo."

"Hey big daddy," she said all jipper and shit. "Why don't you come pick me up after work and…"

"Jovan," I said cutting her bullshit short. "I don't want any confusion as to what I'm about to say, so don't talk just listen.

"It ain't shit between us and it never was. I don't dig you on the vibe you want me to. I'm not trying to hurt your feelings, but I have to keep it gangster."

"Nigga I don't want you," she said just like a woman scorned. "You ain't shit."

"Good, we understand each other."

"Supreme wait," she said swallowing her pride. "What do you want me to do?"

"Don't call me. One," I said and hung up the phone.

I'm hungry like a hostage so I went downstairs to hook up a grub. I ain't give Jovan a second thought because I told her what the deal is. If she causes some drama, her ass is dead. I walked through the living room and hit play on the CD player. Welcome to New York City pumped through my speakers. I went to the island in the kitchen and picked up a peach from the counter. The front door opened and DeShawn walked in carrying three big ass grocery bags. Dezionne walked in behind him so I know she's about to throw down in the kitchen. De closed the door and took her blindfold off. Sure enough she headed to the kitchen.

"Where them dollars at," Dezionne said making me realize I ain't have shit on but black Polo boxers.

"Fuck a dollar nigga pick up fifty," De said walking up beside me.

"What's up Quinn," Dezionne said unpacking the bags. "Are you going to eat?"

"Hell yeah," I said clapping my hands. Dezionne gets down in the kitchen. I wonder if Imani can cook. Damn, I'm assimilating this female to every thought I have. De gave me a pound.

"We know what time it is when it comes to your cooking baby," De said lighting a cigarette.

"Baby," Dezionne said.

"My bad boo." He kissed her cheek and went outside.

I went upstairs and took a shower. From the bathroom to my bedroom, I smelled all types of eggs, home fries, pancakes, and sausage. Dezionne could put Denny's straight out of business. I threw on some Polo sweats and a RW t- shirt and went downstairs. We bust our grub out in the gazebo. Dezionne started feeling nauseous so De carried her upstairs to his over–sized bedroom.

"Dezionne's chilling here tonight," De said sitting back down. "I'm a come back here after the meeting."

"Cool nigga," I said still getting down. I don't play when it comes to a grub. "I'll close the club up tonight."

"Good looking."

We finished our food and I went upstairs to change. I threw on a pair of Polo jeans, with a baby blue Polo shirt, and some white Air Force 2's. De made sure Dezionne was cool and we hopped in the Escalade and rolled out. De rolled two blunts and kept one hand on the CD player remote. Our meeting with the team isn't for another hour so we chilled in Cobb's Creek Park.

"Yo," De said sparking his first blunt." I want to keep this next move on some EL shit."

Damn, De never discounts the team so whatever the move is he's playing that shit real close.

"What's the deal?"

"Look, niggas run they mouth plain and simple," he said

plucking his ashes. "We can't have any heat coming back over what somebody heard. "Check it. Big Time's right hand is this dude named Smoke. He got warrants in Detroit and Atlanta. We tell Blaze to handle Big Time, 5-0 will handle Smoke and their crew falls off."

Yo, De is a mad scientist on some crooked calculating shit.

"That's the bomb plan," I said scratching my head. "What are we going to tell the niggas though?"

De puffed his blunt.

"That dude got us for the okey doke."

Imani

Three months flew by in an unforgettable breeze of Quinnzel, my life long date with destiny. Although he ain't dick me down yet, please believe I am the girl in his movies. Within three months I know more about Quinnzel than brothers I knew for years. That's what I'm looking for. Most men don't share their life story. Usually for one reason, they don't plan on having you around long enough for their world to be relevant. But me and my sexy daddy always bust it up. Sunday, he told me I was fucking with a mobster so he stays on his P's & Q's. That's why I'm not allowed in the back of the club, we don't roll in the EXT, and I'll have to wear a blindfold to his house. I definitely respect him for trying to protect me. And I told him as long as he keeps me safe, he wouldn't wake up dead. Monday, Quinnzel told me he wanted to take me personal. He said he could fulfill my innermost fantasies if I gave him the privilege. May, June, July…I'm watching the sunrise, I'm getting my feet rubbed, and I'm drowning in love. There's nothing I can do about it.

July 3rd, he finally took me to his crib which should be called the Palace. He led me through a black beaded archway with cream and brown beads forming a figure eight.

I sat in a red leather chair with a curved glass swan resting on top.

"Press the button," Quinnzel said in my ear from behind my chair. "But will it be the right button?"

I looked to my right and saw a remote, with three buttons, sitting on a sterling silver table with two crystal champagne glasses and a bowl of chocolate covered strawberries. My feminine wiles told me to push the red button. I pushed the button and the silk curtain I was sitting in front of parted. A disco ball dropped from the ceiling and spun in a tizzy. Imani appeared on the wall in a transparent neon light with glowing stars twirling around my name. Quinnzel walked from behind my chair and took my hand in his. He led me to a star spotlight in the center of the floor. I looked into his hypnotic eyes and we danced to whatever the hell was playing. The music is mute stacked up against my screaming heart. This man lets his actions speak for themselves. Everyday is a pleasure, with Quinnzel showing me he needs me in his life. I haven't been upstairs yet and I can hardly contain my tears. This is the perfect moment to tame three months of yearning.

"Can I keep you," I said stepping away from him.

"Yes."

Quinnzel pulled me close to him and kissed me so delicately, I got dizzy. He bit my neck so soft and sensual, I'm moist. I took his hand and led him upstairs like I live here. The candle lit hall-way led me to his bedroom. I followed a trail of two dozen long stem white roses to his bed. A blanket of pink rose pedals was stretched over his brick red comforter. Quinnzel seductively unbuttoned my Donna Karen blouse, sucking every inch of skin he revealed. He traced the lace trim of my bra with his tongue letting my shirt fall to the floor. Quinnzel turned me around and unbuttoned my skirt sliding his hands inside. He ran his hands over my ass pushing my skirt to the floor. I stepped out of my skirt and lay on his feather soft bed. Quinnzel stood at the foot of the bed and looked upon me with a mystic gaze.

"Turn over."

I turned over on my stomach and he slowly pulled my panties down blessing my ass with juicy kisses and playful bites.

"Umm."

Quinnzel grabbed my legs with his strong ass hands and flipped me over, pulling me to the end of the bed. He got down on his knees and stroked my pussy.

"Do your thing boy. SHIT."

My body erupted, pussy dripping wet. I ground my hips to

the sweet melody of Quinnzel's tongue. Clouds rolled in. I exploded dripping cream in his mouth. My legs twitched in the aftermath, while I struggled to catch my breath. Quinnzel kissed me and I moaned overwhelmed by aching desire. I pulled his shirt over his head and my lips ran ferociously across his solid, chiseled chest. I unbuttoned his RocaWear jeans and slid my hand inside of his silk boxers. I pushed him on the bed and pulled that shit off. He grabbed my arms and laid my body on top of his. Quinnzel caressed my back and unfastened my bra in the same motion. He laid me on the bed and sucked my titties like he was trying to get Robitussin out them muthfuckas. I trembled feeling the tip of his dick penetrating. I hollered in ecstasy, climaxing with every stroke. The depth and thickness of his manhood left permanent imprints inside me. I cried and kissed him everywhere I felt skin. Quinnzel licked the streaming tears of pure pleasure from my cheeks. Just as he was about to come, I rolled him over and rode his tremendous dick like a cowboy at a rodeo. He called for the Lord feeling that last nut come. Quinnzel flipped me over and wiped his sweaty forehead against mine. We slept in the calm after our storm.

Quinnzel and I spent the 4th of July at Dorney Park with DeShawn and Dezionne, and the rest of the weekend in each other's arms. I am grateful to have a man who knows exactly what I need to make me whole, so I can smile again. Mrs. Tamia Grant Hill, you go girl because those are my sentiments exactly. There were eight messages from daddy and five from Cierra waiting for me when I got home late Sunday night. Both of them were cursing me out for disappearing for five days. I picked up the phone to call Daddy, but got in the bed instead. Angels kissed my eyelids welcoming Quinnzel into my dreams. He's yummy. I dreamed so hard, I over slept Monday morning. I jumped up, threw on my midnight blue Louis Vuitton suit and slipped into my tan Fendi shoes. I grabbed my tan Coach bag and neck scarf from the closet and jetted. I got a two-way from my baby while I was parking, telling me he's taking me to lunch. That's what's up. I flew off the elevator and down the hall to my suite.

"Good Morning Imani," Jovan said sipping a cup of coffee.

I poured a glass of cran-apple juice and walked over to her desk.

"Good Morning."

Jovan passed me my messages grinning from ear to ear.

"Are you okay," I said sipping my juice.

"I had a date last night," she said dancing in her chair.

"That's good," I said walking to my office.

I didn't ask any questions. I never mix business with personals. Classic advice, I'd learned over the years. I sat in my office all morning finalizing my power point presentation for tomorrow's meeting with Sixers' management. If they accept my proposal, my plan will definitely come together. I didn't realize what time it was until Jovan buzzed my phone.

"Your lunch date is here," she said with much bass in her voice.

"Escort him in."

Jovan flung open my door and stormed in my office. Quinnzel walked in behind her. Jovan's venomous stare pierced me. Her heated tension swarmed around me as she held her position at the door. What the hell is wrong with her?

"Is there anything else Jovan," I said standing up from my desk.

She held her stance a second longer, then left. My man kissed me and immediately erased the nonsense. A pink stripped Victoria secret bag dangled in his hand.

"What's in the bag," I asked tickling his ear with my tongue. He moaned.

"A gift."

"For who?" He kissed me.

"Me."

Quinnzell Supreme Sharpe

Jovan's stupid ass drew on some bullshit yesterday. I knew it was a matter time. But Imani handled it like a champ. She boldly enforced her position minus the rah-rah shit. That's what I'm talking about. Damn, I dig everything about this woman. I know what she wants, because she knows what she wants. It's that simple. And Imani definitely throws that shit on me crazy in the bedroom, with no question. She made my body scream out yeah yeah yeah. I say bend over, she says round 2. That's my flavor all day. I'm hooking up a surprise weekend chill-a-way to celebrate Imani signing the 76ERS to a contract. My lady is about to blow up. I ain't talk to AI since he went through that bullshit scandal with his wiz and the media, but I'm a holla at him to get the inside scoop on what they really think of my baby girl. Damn, I'm laying here bullshitting when I need to pick Dezionne up from the doctor's. She hasn't been feeling well, so they want to make sure it's nothing wrong with her that could hurt the baby. She and Imani are cool as shit too. They're always bussing it up on the horn, going to plays and concerts and whatnot. I'm definitely feeling that.

I rolled out and got to Temple University Hospital about one o'clock. I thought Dezionne would be waiting outside, but I had to park and go get her. I asked the receptionist what room she was in, but she ain't hear me because she was so busy watching my ice.

"What was that sexy," she said leaning forward so her titties were on the counter. I'm not intrigued; Imani got plenty titty.

"Dezionne Sinclair, what room," I said with frustration so she could see I'm not trying to dig up on her. She's not hearing me though.

"Are you a relative," she asked rubbing my arm with her crusty hands. I snatched my hand from under hers.

"Brother. And I don't have time to play your games."

She laughed nonchalantly like she ain't know I dissed her and picked up Dezionne's file. Her whole attitude went flip mode when she read the cover sheet.

"You're going to have to speak with the doctor," she said.

I stood there with the dummy look while she paged Dr. Johnson. She didn't make eye contact with me again. What the fuck is going on? The doctor came out and told me when Dezionne came in she was hemorrhaging. He rushed her to emergency and did a sonogram. The baby was making no moves and he couldn't find a heartbeat. My mind went blank.

"What does all that mean man?"

"We're going to have to deliver a stillborn. I'm sorry," he said patting my shoulder. "The nurse will bring you back after you notify your family."

He walked away and left me standing there stinking. My heart is crying, my mind is racing, and I can't stop my fucking hands from shaking. I'm lost. I want to call De, but what the fuck am I supposed to say? I called Imani. Her voice calmed my steaming soul. She told me to call Dezionne's people; she would call De, and be here in a minute. Where the fuck is De at anyway? As soon as the thought crossed my mind, De's code popped up on my two-way. I know he ain't talk to Imani yet so I didn't call him back. I told Dezionne's mom what was up and she broke down on the phone. Damn, I never question any decision God makes, but this is fucked up. I waited in a corner by myself in a daze. In a half an hour the family had filled the hallways. My heart ached to see DeShawn and Mrs. Bonnie crying together. Imani hugged me close, like she was trying to steal my pain.

"I love you." I realized that was my first time saying those three words, and I can't wait to say them a million times over. Imani smiled through her tears.

"I'm in love with you too," she replied.

After the longest two hours of our lives, the doctor came out and told us Dezionne was in recovery. They had to cut her open to take the baby, so she's still knocked out. DeShawn and Mrs. Bonnie were the first to go see her. They held hands walking down the hallway, but Mrs. Bonnie crumbled and she collapsed to the floor. Dezionne is her only daughter so I know she's going through it.

"Why Lord why," she cried out beating her hands on the cold hard tile.

I ran down the hall to help De help her up. Imani followed, and nurses were coming from the other direction. Mrs. Bonnie cried in fury, bringing tears to all of our eyes. My brother kneeled on the floor and bowed his head. I know he's asking for strength and guidance. He gathered himself and stood up.

"De, I..."

He shook his head telling me there's no need for words. I hugged my brother and we cried together. At nine o' clock, visiting hours were over. Mrs. Bonnie and De stayed and I went to Imani's crib.

I was drowning. My lungs were submerged by gallons of water. I coughed up blood and felt my chest caving. I heard my heart beat fading. I tried to swim to the surface, but thousands of infants were chained to my ankles. A faceless child appeared and reached its hand out for mine. Before I could get a grip, the child swam away. I yelled come back but my voice was trapped in my throat. I'm sinking.

"Hush its okay baby," Imani said wiping my sweaty face with a damp cloth.

Damn, what the fuck was that about? I'm tripping. I laid my head in Imani's lap. She didn't ask any questions, she just held me.

I woke up to a plate of eggs, grits, and bacon stacked up on a tray with a white rose. I grubbed, found my boxers, and got up. I walked up behind Imani and wrapped my arms around her tight waist. She leaned her head against my chest and I kissed her neck.

"Where are you going," I asked sliding my hands inside of her zebra print Victoria Secret nightgown.

"Nowhere if you need me to stay."

She turned around and kissed me. Damn, this woman is my life's love. Her kiss puts my soul at ease. I didn't tell her about my nightmare because I never told her about my seed. I don't want to hold no secrets from Imani so I need to break this shit down. I thought she would feel some type of way about me not saying shit until now. But after I broke it down, she was more concerned than upset.

"Did she have the baby?"

"I guess so."

"Was she really pregnant?"

"I don't know. I never thought she was lying."

"Q, females can be real spiteful creatures when an opportunity presents itself," she said and kissed my forehead.

"Damn, you actually fucked my head up."

I started piecing shit together.

"I just don't want you to be naïve," she said and got up from the couch. I followed her to the bedroom.

"Good looking," I said feeling on her booty. "Imani, I will never…"

She put her finger to my lips and shook her head.

"I know."

Imani didn't make it to work that morning. She was my love slave instead. At twelve o' clock, we met the Fam at the hospital to check Dezionne out. Mrs. Bonnie is taking care of all of the funeral arrangements so Double D has no worries on that note. De wheeled Dezionne to the car and we went to Mrs. Bonnie's crib in Elkins Park for lunch. It was the most depressing meal of my life. Dezionne rubbed her stomach and started crying. It was downhill from there. Mrs. Bonnie started crying and Imani even threw in some whimpers. Sunday's funeral may be too much for me to handle. Mrs. Bonnie said Dezionne needed her rest so De carried her upstairs. They're staying here until after the burial, so De went to Dezionne's crib to get some clothes. I stayed at Imani's crib so I wouldn't be too far if Double D needs me. I went to the Palace every morning at five to count the paper and close up.

Sunday, the club didn't open. Thunderous storm clouds filled the sky pouring rain over our already dreary day. The funeral was closed casket and only two pallbearers were needed to carry the one-foot long coffin. Pain filled tears stained the earth when Baby- boy Sharpe was laid to rest.

Imani

Dezionne barricaded herself at her moms' house for two months after the funeral, not that I blame her. I could never imagine burying my child. I called her everyday and brought her flowers every week for the first month. Our conversation was meek when I was there and she was always happy to see me. Yesterday I told her, when she felt up to it, I would take her to an all day spa where island men will pamper us. That brought a smile to her weary face. I wish there was something more I could do to console her.

I spent Friday evening at the office reviewing and outlining the research I compiled through training camp and pre-season. With the regular season weeks away my schedule is full with one-on-one interviews with everyone listed on the 76ERS roster and my meeting with the NBA commissioner. You know I do it way big. He heard my corporate clause is bout it bout it from the Sixers front office and wants to sign me to an exclusive contract, which will allow me to prep all players at the NBA drafts. I am also hoping to assemble a WNBA team for Philly, tentatively named the Philadelphia Spirit or Charms. I love it when a plan comes together.

I went to the copy room to fax the finalized schedule. Jovan stared at me as I walked through the vestibule and if looks could kill, I'd be dead. I honestly have no idea what her beef with me is but for the last couple of months she's had hate in her blood. On a professional level, Jovan has an extremely lucrative deal. And with the moves I'm making now the future is nothing but promising. It can't be personal because my personal life is completely private and separate from all of my business endeavors.

Jovan followed me in the copy room and slammed a stack of files on the table. I had enough of this.

"Jovan, is there a problem?"

"Yeah. What's up with you and Supreme?"

"Jovan," I said calmly. "I don't know anyone named Supreme."

"Oh you're going to play me like I'm stupid," she said. "I saw you pushing his Boni out King of Prussia. He comes all up and through here smiling in your face with flowers and gifts and shit. Leaving love notes and candy. What's up with that?"

"Q," I said with a bizarre look on my face. I know she's not questioning me about my dude.

"So his name begins with a Q," she said drumming her fingers on the glass tabletop. "What's the rest of it?"

"You don't know his name," I said holding back my laughter. How silly does homegirl sound? "Did you really think his name was Supreme?"

"Fuck you Imani," she said fighting to hold back her tears. "You think you're the shit because you drive a Bentley and you got this little corporation…"

"Let me stop this right now," I said approaching her. "If this about Q, then keep it about him. Don't you dare downplay my accomplishments over a man who thinks so little of you he didn't even tell you his real name. Oh and let's not forget Jovan you work for me."

"I don't have to take this shit."

"That's right you don't," I said fuming. "Good-bye Jovan."

Damn, Quinnzel was right, good-bye is forever. Jovan smacked the file folders off of the table and they fell to the floor. She probably planned that shit. I cracked the hell up after she stormed out. I know Jovan sings and swings at the Palace but I'm not pressed. I trust Quinnzel. And since she doesn't know his name, it can't be that serious. I bent down to pick up my files and the phone rang. I ran to my now empty assistant station to answer it.

"Good evening, thank you for calling Miracle Media."

"Imani, its Dezionne."

"Hey girl, how are you doing?"

"Hungry," she said laughing. "Dinner at Red Lobster?"

"No doubt. I'll pick you up in a half."

I gathered my files from the floor, grabbed my jacket and bag from my office, and rolled. I got down to the garage and saw Jovan and two other chicks leaning against my car. This bitch thinks it's a game. I pulled my pepper spray from my bag and approached my ride. I stopped right in front of Jovan.

"Are you serious Jovan?"

"No words Imani."

The two girls charged me from the left. With three sprays, I gave both of those bitches' cataracts. I two-pieced Jovan in the nose and stomach and her knees buckled. I kicked her stupid ass in the mouth and called security.

Dezionne and I laughed about that shit over a bottomless bucket of snow crab legs. She sympathized and offered to help me in the office until I find a new assistant. Damn Jovan. I dropped Dezionne off at ten-thirty and went home. After an hour-long bubble bath I went to bed. The phone rang at twelve o' clock pissing me the hell off. I yanked the phone off of the night table.

"Who the hell is this?"

"Come out to the balcony."

"Baby?" I sat up and turned my light to its softest setting. "Let me ask…"

"Hush, come out on the balcony."

I put on my robe and went outside. A glistening white stretch Hummer rolling on iced out twenty-fours pulled up beneath me.

"Pack a bag and meet me outside."

"I'm coming."

I grabbed my newest laciest secrets, my essentials, three outfits, and flew out of the door. It didn't dawn on me that I only had on a robe until two little boys passed me in the hallway. I excited their chest hairs with one glance. That gives me an idea. I ran back down the hall to my apartment. I put a full-length leather coat on over my pink satin backless thin strapped night-gown, laced my Dolce&Gabanna sandals up my calf and ran back down the hall to the elevator.

The driver opened the door and I stepped inside. Damn, Gucci seats, Fendi interior. A dozen long stem white roses sat on the couch opposite Quinnzel. He looks scrumptious in his cream Polo sweater and brown leather jacket. Damn, my man is always dressed like he's straight out of GQ.

"I need to tell you something," he said tenderly kissing me.

I sat back in my seat and looked at him. He held onto my stare and pushed a button on the window panel. Ginuwine's Differences seeped through the speakers. The music changed to RL's Good Man, and Quinnzel's eyes never left mine.

"No words can describe how much I love you Imani," Quinnzel said kissing my hands. "And I never want to lose this feeling."

R. Kelly's If I Could Explain the Joy I Feel played next and Quinnzel hugged me with so much compassion tears emerged. I fell asleep in his arms until we reached the surprise destination. And in his arms I found forever. I could spend eternity safe in Quinnzel's sweet embrace. It was two o' clock in the morning when we arrived at our beachfront villa in Ocean City, Maryland.

I took my shoes off and went over to the window. I pulled back the curtains and let the gleaming light from the crescent moon beam inside. Hundreds of stars twinkled in the night sky reflecting on the dark ocean waters. I unlocked the door and went out on the balcony. I inhaled the crisp night air and hoped the day's bullshit would escape when I exhaled because I am defi-nitely not fucking this night up with stories of Jovan. Q walked up behind me and turned me around. I love the way his arms fit perfectly in the small of my back. The profound expression on his face glowed in the moonlight. He looked in my eyes like he's searching for a lost treasure in a moonless night.

"Close your eyes," he whispered.

I smiled at him and closed my eyes. Quinnzel traced my neckline with his fingertips. I felt a cool sensation replace his touch.

"It's the key to my heart."

I opened my eyes to see a platinum key etched with diamonds dangling from a twelve-inch platinum bone.

"Q..."

He erased the rest of my words with a kiss. I moaned. His lips, so soft so juicy. Damn. We filled the cool night air with our passionate heat. Mounds of pleasure erupted between us.

"I want to show you something," he said stealing a final kiss.

Shit, at this moment his every wish is my command. Quinnzel took my hand and led me out to the beach. Crashing waves carried rushing water to the shore. We walked, hand in hand, barefoot across the sand.

"Oh baby," I said as we walked up to his magnificent work of art.

Resting in a lounge chair, under a tent, was a masterfully painted motif of my mom. Her name scrolled in bold calligraphy across the bottom. My welding crocodile tears blinded me. He must've gotten the picture from my apartment, but I didn't ask any questions. I already know everything I need to. There is no need for words. I'm standing on the beach with the man I would give the breath I breathe. I have a wicked desire to taste his manhood.

"I want to make you feel good."

I pushed Quinnzel down in the sand and sable and took all of our clothes off. I killed his dick softly with my tongue. The slow grind in his hips cosigned my chivy. Quinnzel licked my fingers and smacked my ass.

"Nobody has ever made me feel like this," he said shivering.

Quinnzel laid me down and the blaze of our fiery sentiment melted the sand beneath us. A cool breeze caressed our sweaty bodies, but it damn sure didn't douse the flame. I moaned getting dizzy. Quinnzel bit my shoulder.

"Yes," I uttered licking his lips.

We made love until Heaven shined a light on us.

Saturday we drove to a crab feast at Baltimore's Harbor. We ate, shopped, and danced on the boardwalk. Busch Garden was the next stop and we spent another bliss filled evening on the beach. Sunday came too soon and we were driving back to Philly. I lay in Quinnzel's lap on the ride home. Our weekend was perfect, but for some reason Friday kept repeating itself in my mind. I mean, damn, this Jovan bitch waited for me at my car to fight. Something is missing from this story. Quinnzel noticed my sudden uneasy mood.

"What's up," he said twirling my hair around his fingers.

"I fought Jovan on Friday."

"Y'all boxed?" He sat up.

"I beat her ass and gave her two girlfriends handicap plates."

"I don't believe this shit," he said pulling a Corona from the bar. "I'm a handle this okay?"

"Handle what, Quinnzel?"

He rubbed the bridge of his nose.

"Jovan was digging up on me for a minute but I never dealt with her."

"And you wait until now to tell me that."

"Do you want me to break down profiles on every female I knew before you were given to me, because I will."

"No Q that's not what I want," I said lowering my tone to quiet the hype. "I trust you, so I know all of the females from your past are way back there. But when they show up in our world, in my face you got to dead that shit. I should never have to defend myself from any female over you."

"You're right Queen, I apologize."

"I accept."

"So, did you box her head off?" I gave Quinnzel a pound.

"I split that bitch to the white meat. Flawless victory."

Quinnzel fell on the floor laughing. We laughed and joked for the rest of the ride home. The limo pulled into my complex around five o' clock. My heart dropped to my feet when the driver opened the door and I saw Cierra sitting on the steps to my building.

Quinnzell Supreme Sharpe

Imani jumped out of the car when she saw her girlfriend sitting on the steps. She's a butter pecan pretty chick. Her face looks real familiar to me too. A message from De popped up on my two-way telling me to meet him at the office in an hour. I got out of the car to give Imani her bags so I could roll out. Imani whispered something to her girl and they both smiled while she waved at me. I know her from somewhere. I waved back and picked Imani's bags up off the floor. They walked over to the car and as soon as she introduced herself, sirens went off in my head. I tried to hide the rage that was rapidly boiling inside of me. I told Imani I had to bounce and knew she sensed my anxiety. She rushed to me.

"Baby what's wrong?"

"It's her."

I threw Imani's shit on the ground. Everything went black and my nightmares flashed before my eyes. My mind surged like wildfire.

"Where is my seed Cierra?" I growled.

Imani searched my eyes for an answer without asking a question. My hostility showed the truth and Imani's face turned to stone.

"Oh my God," Cierra said backing away from us. "Supreme."

Imani whirled around and faced Cierra. I know she's aching, but this isn't about her. I ice grilled Cierra, clenching my teeth so hard sparks flew.

"I'm a ask you one more time, where is my child?"

I stepped around Imani and approached Cierra. I wished she was a dude, so I could beat the shit out of her.

"I don't have any kids," she said stepping back.

I know she's terrified. She has no idea about what I'm capable of doing.

"You had an abortion?"

Cierra looked at Imani with tears forming in her eyes. Imani didn't say a word. She just picked up her bags and went inside.

"You want the truth?"

"Fuck do you think?"

"I wasn't pregnant," Cierra said crying. "I just needed money but when you wanted me to keep the baby I was salty."

Is this a grown ass woman talking? I stood right in front of her and she started shaking.

"You are a trifling bitch," I said. "And if you were a dude, I'd beat you down."

I spit in Cierra's face and got in the car. I called Imani and apologized to her for acting all crazy. I told her I loved her and I would holla later. Before she hung up, I told Imani not to get involved.

I tried to get my mind right before I got to the spot. Damn, I don't believe that bitch. See that's why most niggas treat females like shit without a second thought. They're figuring shorty is going to pull some off the wall shit anyway. But yo, cut that short, tricks are for kids. Grown ass people shouldn't play games. I pulled up to the Palace at seven. I paid my young bull for driving and went around back. De was shooting pool by himself.

"Yo peoples," I said pulling a Corona from the bar. "What's the business?"

"What's the deal my nigga? You look like shit, trouble in Paradise?"

De lit a cigarette.

"Not in Paradise, in the back yard," I said sitting on the couch. "Jovan from the left, my fake-ass baby mom from my right. These chicks are ill."

"Say word." De walked over to the couch and sat next to me.

"Imani fucked Jovan up and fired her, and her best fucking

friend is the broad from Georgetown who said she was knocked up with my seed. That bitch was lying."

"Bitch?"

"Bitch."

"Damn."

"And through the bullshit, me and Imani are riding with no brakes."

"That's the deal," De said splitting a Dutch. "But check this out. Word on the street is some Georgia niggas is asking about us."

"Where this shit come from? We been on the low since we made that last move."

"Niggas is trying to open up shop at the late Big Time's set."

"What it's hitting for?"

"Rahiem is going to holla at me later." De sparked his chronic up.

Nino and Cash came in with Ox Tails, rice and peas. We grubbed and decided if these niggas want beef, we're going to war. Cream on the block is crazy since we took Big Time off the map. Ain't nobody fucking that up, especially not some out of town niggas. We're going to show them niggas how 215 get down with some extreme hot shit. Nino already hit Monster up and told him to keep the heavy artillery on stand-by.

Tonight Dezionne is coming back to the club for the first time since the funeral. So De is coming back here after he holla at Rahiem. I went to the crib to chill for a minute, but I told De I would come back through. Nino and Cash went to the block to clock shit. I got to my crib at ten o' clock. I went in my room and took my clothes off. I took a shower and got in the bed. My mind is on Imani but I know she's with that bitch. I said fuck it and called her anyway. When she answered the phone it sound like she was crying.

"What's wrong , baby."

"Me and Cierra went through it after you called," she said sniffling. "She left and I don't know where she is."

I feel bad for my lady going through it with her friend over me. My other line beeped before I could say anything.

"Hold on Queen," I said switching the line. "Hello."

"Quinnzel, its Darren."

"What's going on Mr. D?"

Me and Imani's pops are cool as shit. He invited me to play chess when I first met Imani. He broke down life and showed me his sawed off shot guns. I like his style.

"Have you talked to Nae?"

"She's on the line now."

"You tell her Cierra is here and she's leaving tomorrow," he said sternly. "Don't let my daughter worry herself over this high-class dame. She ain't no good, never has been."

"Yes sir."

"And son," he said in tone that let me know he cared. "Don't you pay Cierra no never mind. Women like her are only here to test your manhood. If you pass, you'll find the woman who will make your toes curl and your body shake."

"What happens if you fail?"

"I don't believe Imani will ever let you find out. And if it ain't broke don't fix it. Good night son."

"Good night Mr. Darren."

Damn, so all the years I spent dealing with bullshit females gave me the knowledge to recognize my Queen. That's some deep shit. I hung up the phone and it rang right back.

"Hello."

"Baby, what happened?"

Oh shit, I'm so gone I forgot Imani was even on the phone.

"My bad love, that was your pops."

"What did he say?"

"I told him I love you to death Imani," I said smiling. "And that I would never let you feel an ounce of hurt. I'm on my way to get you."

Me and Imani went to a late night movie and had breakfast at Michael's. I brought her back to my house and gave her a full body hot oil massage. We made love in the Jacuzzi and I held Imani while she slept. My two-way went off at five o' clock. It was De telling me he's pulling into the garage and to meet him outside. I got out of bed and covered Imani's smooth honey-colored body. I threw on some sweats and went downstairs. De was smoking a blunt in the gazebo.

"What's up family," I said yawning.

I sat down and De gave me a pound.

"The top dog of the Georgia bulls is this cat named Lucifer."

I thought for a minute and a bomb went off in my head.

"Nino's cousin Lucifer?"

"Hell yeah. You don't forget when you meet a muthfucka named Lucifer."

"What the fuck?"

"I don't know Fam," De said smoking. "But shit is about to get real greasy."

Imani

Yo, I'm still tripping off of Cierra. She had the audacity to come at my neck like I lied and said she was pregnant. I never thought of begrudging Cierra's sistership over her shit with Quinnzel. But if it's fuck me Sis, no it's fuck you. Damn. Ten years is a long time to forget. Daddy told me in high school, Cierra was a dolled up dummy. I'll be damned if it wasn't some truth behind that statement. But I can't front like losing my friend doesn't hurt.

Anyway since the 76ERS home opener against Milwaukee me and Dezionne got business pumping at Miracle Media; It's murder. And thanks to her brilliant idea to sponsor youth programs, we now have community support. Dezionne's motherly smile glows from Monday to Thursday at the newly renovated East Germantown recreation center. She assembled a learning camp teaching basic math and vocabulary. With gym, arts, dance, crafts, and drama as our after day program. Dezionne is organizing a talent showcase as an end of season celebration. And of course we're kicking it at every home game with our children of Club Synergy.

After an extremely productive week, we left the office at twelve on Friday to do a little shopping. We hit up Victoria's Secret in the Liberty Place and I copped a leather RocaWear jacket for Quinnzel from City Blue. After lunch at Chick Filet, I drove to the Palace so Dezionne could pick up the money she had to deposit.

"Hurry up girl," I said pulling up to the front of the club.

"Come on Imani, walk me to the office."

"I already told you Quinnzel said I'm not allowed back there."

"That's sweet now bring your ass on," she said getting out of my car.

I shook my head. What's the worst that could happen? I got out and we walked around back.

"Pour yourself a drink," Dezionne said. She moved the wall mounted picture that covers the latch for the safe.

I sat on the couch with my drink while Dezionne counted her money. Damn, this office is laid out. I heard voices approaching and looked over to Dezionne.

"Shit," she said when DeShawn and Quinnzel walked in. "Busted."

"Baby I…"

"What are you hard-headed or something?" Quinnzel asked walking over to me.

I have no excuses. I just looked at him with pouty lips and my puppy-dog face. He laughed.

"Come on, let's go."

"Dezionne I'll call you later punk," I said following Quinnzel.

She crossed her eyes and stuck her tongue out at me. Quinnzel stopped at the door.

"Beautiful, I asked you not to come back here for a reason."

"Baby I didn't mean to disrespect you," I said leaning my body against his. I felt a throb in his love muscle. "It will never happen again."

I kissed Quinnzel and his body melted into mine. It's amazing how love conquers all. There's no use in fussing and fighting.

He opened the door and a black tinted out Jeep pulled up. Quinnzel yelled squad and pulled two snug-nose 357 magnums from underneath his trench coat. DeShawn broke from the office cradling a Mac10 in each armpit. Quinnzel pushed me on the floor and a barrage of bullets rained above me. I covered my head caught in an instance of terror. Through my tears, I saw a reflection of Terrell's image falling in my lap. Damn, it was a dead body! I heard a car door slam and tires screeching. The guns stopped firing and DeShawn went outside. I lay shaking on the floor. Quinnzel picked me up and held me. DeShawn drug Cash's corpse inside. His hands were bound and his mouth duck taped. Cash was shot six times in the chest like he was executed and his throat was slit from ear to ear. Damn, four babies call this man daddy. Quinnzel whispered something to DeShawn and took me home.

I left my keys for Dezionne to bring me my ride. DeShawn told her to run through the hidden passage in the office before the shooting. I said nothing to Quinnzel on the ride to my house. I just sat in bewilderment. All I'm thinking is that could have been Quinnzel them niggas threw from that Jeep. I know reality is, we are all going to die, but death is not one of my aspirations. And I'm in love with a man, who apparently, doesn't care whether he lives or dies. Damn, my mind is playing tricks on me. We pulled up to my building and went inside. Quinnzel sat on the couch and watched me pace the floor.

"Relax your mind Imani."

"That could have been you all shot the fuck up," I said glaring at him.

"I can't change the game up now."

"And I can't bury another love one." I sat in my fluffy chair and put my hands over my face.

"If you would've followed directions, we wouldn't be having this conversation."

That was a foolish thing to say. I glared at Quinnzel like he was stupid.

"So as long as I don't see you get killed, its okay?"

"I told you what it was from jump," he said sharply. "My life is not a game."

"And mine is?"

"No," Quinnzel said grilling me. "Meaning together we have to be serious and pay attention."

"So you think I'm a game?"

"I think you're not even hearing me right now."

Quinnzel's two-way went off signaling time-out, just in time to save face.

"Look, baby, I have to go." He kissed me like he never touched me. "I'll be back tonight."

"So long Supreme."

"Imani don't do that," he said frowning. "I have NEVER been Supreme to you. I'm out."

He left and I stood there feeling like a dickhead. I know I hurt him and that wasn't my intention. But I know Supreme will be our downfall.

I poured a drink and called Dezionne's cell phone.

"What's the deal Sis?"

"I need a drink," I said sipping on E&J and coke.

"I'm on my way to your crib."

"Cool."

I waited outside for Dezionne to pull up. She drove and we wound up at Jillians in the Franklin Mills Mall sipping margaritas and eating Buffalo wings and potato skins. I know Dezionne knows I feel some type of way.

"Rest your mind Nae," she said licking her fingers. "De and Quinn will handle it."

"Is it that easy?"

"They're hustlers but they're smart," she said. "They're businessmen."

I rolled my eyes.

"Imani, Quinnzel will never let anything happen to you. That was the first time any nigga brought animosity to the club, and I know it will be the last."

"Who were those guys?"

Dezionne stopped eating and looked at me. I know I'm asking the wrong question, but I don't give a damn.

"Dezionne?"

"Listen, Nino is one piece of the team. I don't know when he fell off but, he's a done deal after today." She sipped her drink. "DeShawn is not going to let this ride. So you need to leave it alone. Trust me Nae, and believe me when I tell you Quinnzel loves you to death. I know because I know him."

She winked at me and finished her margarita.

"Round two," I said finally smiling.

"Hook it up. Imani," Dezionne said peeping behind me. "Dude is checking you out early. Don't turn around he's coming over here."

"Excuse me ladies," the familiar voice said. "Imani is that you?"

I looked up to see Derek standing over me.

"What's up stranger?"

"Nothing much," he said holding my hand. "You look beautiful as always Imani."

"Thank you," I said trying not to blush. "Derek, this is Dezionne."

"Nice to meet you Derek."

"The pleasure is all mine Dezionne," he said giving her crazy rhythm when he spoke. "Imani it was good seeing you again."

Derek kissed my cheek.

"Call me, Imani."

We watched Derek walk away.

"Okay cupcake, get him killer," Dezionne said slapping me five. "Let me find out."

"It ain't shit. He's boring as hell and can't kiss worth a damn."

"Oh no, that's a terrible thing."

"Please believe me."

We cracked up. Dezionne and I chilled for another hour or so then I took her home. DeShawn's Jaguar was parked behind Dezionne's Lexus.

"I'll talk to you tomorrow girl," she said hugging me before she got out. "Remember what I said."

"Later Sis."

I waited for Dezionne to get inside before I pulled off. I got home around nine o' clock, hoping Quinnzel would be there. I opened the door and was greeted only by dim lights. I took off my shoes and went in the bedroom. No Quinnzel. I went out on the balcony. Still no Quinnzel. I came inside and sat on the couch. As soon as I sent Quinnzel a two-way the phone rang.

"Hello."

"Is this Imani Best?"

"Yes, who is this?"

"I'm afraid I have some news for you."

My heart hit the floor. No God please. I closed my teary eyes and said a silent prayer.

"Ms. Best," the voice said in a whisper. "Love will be waiting at home."

"I'm in love with you."

I dropped the phone and turned around. Quinnzel appeared in my doorway. I raised my head to the ceiling and said thank You.

Quinnzell Supreme Sharpe

I found solace in the hot tub after I bust it up with my lady for a minute. Me and De told the family her heart couldn't handle the funeral, so it wasn't a thing that she ain't come. My miz feels the same way Imani does about thug life and the street, drugs and guns. But Imani was cool before the shootout. It ain't about nothing though because I understand her mental. Last night, she gave me a card with the same words that I wrote to her a month of Sunday's ago. One line in particular got me to thinking: tomorrow is a mystery. On some really real shit I don't give a fuck about my tomorrow if Imani is not a part of it. I actually love this woman with every fiber of my being. I'm stronger with Imani than I ever was alone. My miz always told me my lady would lead my fate by saving my life and romancing me with the first kiss. Tonight, I told her Imani embraced my kingdom proving she is my future wife. I got out of the hot tub, oiled my body, and got in my bed ass-hole naked. I'm feening for Imani and my succulent taffy. I reached over to grab the phone and the business line rang. I switched the inbound lines.

"Yo."

"Pussy you're going to die tonight."

"Word."

"Kiss that sexy bitch good-bye nigga. I'm a wax that ass when you're gone."

Click. Boom.

I slammed the phone down and jumped up.

"Shawn." I ran downstairs.

De was in the game-room playing Grand Theft Auto in his

boxers and shit.

"Yo, nigga get dressed."

"What's the deal baby boss?"

"Niggas just called here on some murder one shit."

"Oh hell no," De said throwing the joystick on the floor. "I'm a get dressed, we're going to hit that nigga Blaze up and tell him to set the plan in motion."

"Hurry the fuck up dude."

De looked at me all crazy.

"Nigga, you're butt ass naked, how you going to tell me to hurry the fuck up."

We both got dressed and boned out. We rolled in the Ford F150 De copped on the low when he found out Nino sold his soul. Shit, that nigga took out one of his mans. We ain't going out like that. I hipped all of our soldiers to the game. They know not to fuck with Nino or his peoples. And if that nigga roll up, he's getting shot on the spot.

I told Blaze to meet us in Aubury Park at midnight. We picked up Imani and Dezionne and took them to the Marriott Towne Place Suites in Horsham. Before I rolled Imani kissed me like her heart depended on it. She told me she loved me through sleep-filled eyes. It saddened me to know I made it unsafe for my woman to sleep in her own bed. I'm supposed to be her protector, not bring danger to her. I'm ass backwards and Imani is riding with me like my shit is on point. I ain't say shit on the ride down 611 but De knows what I'm going through. He pulled a blunt from his inner jacket pocket and passed it to me. Damn. I sparked that shit and was fucked up with the first puff of hydro. By the time we got to the park, I was groovy. Blaze was posted up in the woods in all black looking like a shadow. See, that's why I stopped smoking weed. That shit be having me geeking.

"Blaze this is what we need," De said passing him pictures of Nino and his cousins.

De lit a cigarette and Blaze used the light to look at the flicks. His eyes widened when he saw Nino, but he ain't say shit.

He didn't even look surprised.

"Five niggas- twenty g's a head," I said. "Literally."

"I want the fingers of Nino's peoples delivered to him," De said. He puffed his cigarette. "Then bring his bitch ass to me. Hit me up and I'll let you know where to meet us."

"Extra change for the special delivery," I said and tossed Blaze a bag with a hundred grand already in it. "Early."

Me and De walked down Stockton Road and chilled on Price Street. This was a hot strip before operation safe streets went in affect. Now, it's dead as a muthfucka out here. 5-0 got this shit on lock. Ain't nobody eating.

Damn, its two' o clock. It shouldn't take Blaze long to get them niggas though. Like De said before, they run their mouths. Before shit went down, Nino told Bilal his peoples were staying at the Sheraton because his baby mom is staying with him up in the Northeast out Byberry Road. At three-thirty a message popped in De's two-way: It's done. He replied, dumpster, and we rolled out. Blaze dropped a duffel bag at my feet and sat on the trunk of his car. I kicked the bag and four decapitated heads rattled together. Blaze added his own flavor and torched the bodies with acid.

"Pull that pussy out," De said.

Blaze got up and pulled Nino out of the trunk. He had a bloody pillowcase over his head. He fell on the ground and De took the sack off of his head. He stomped on Nino's face until his leg was weak.

"Back up niggas," De said and pissed on Nino's damn near lifeless body.

"Make that fool suffer Blaze. We're out."

I gave Blaze another bag with a hundred stacks and we rolled out. Respect the game. We went to Dezionne's crib to shower and change.

The sun was coming up by the time we made it back to Horsham. We parked at the Marriott and went to our rooms. My Queen was probably up flipping her wig worrying about me and shit. I crept through the darkness and sat in the bedside chair to watch Imani sleep. I smiled looking at my angel for a few moments, until her two-way vibrated on the nightstand next to me. Damn, judgment day like a muthfucka. Trust my lady or check the number? This shit makes me want to holla. I put myself in Imani's position. We would definitely be beefing if she monitored my shit. I mean, I ain't on no collab shit with any females but it's the principalities in this. That's my answer right there, don't fuck with it.

Imani laughed, and her eyes fluttered in a dream. She smiled and her hips started rocking. I know muthfucking well she's dreaming about big daddy long stroke. My dick tingled with mere excitement of the thought. Taffy is my instant pleasure principal. Imani called my name and I definitely knew I made the right decision. Until, her muthfucking two-way went off again. Who the fuck is blowing Imani up all crazy? I forwarded the number to my two-way and stored it in my memory. I'm a holla back on this one, damn that.

I stripped down to my boxers and got in the bed. I cuddled up on Imani's onion booty; makes you want to suck her daddy's dick. She wrapped my arm around her and I kissed her neck. Imani turned over and opened her eyes.

"Are you okay?"

I slid my hand over her cheek. She kissed my fingers as I ran them across her lips.

"Yes."

I kissed Imani's forehead and she closed her eyes. I lay there thinking. It's hot as shit on the block right now. Niggas could come at us at any time. Before I met my tenderoine, I didn't care if I lived or died. Now, I want a future because I think I found my wife.

Imani

It's been a minute since Quinnzel spooked me with our middle of the night get-a-way. Since then, we've been kicking it on the dolo drama free. He and Amir's been riding out too, like every Friday night. That's what's up. Quinnzel's mom came up for Thanksgiving so me and Dezionne got to show off our chef skills. I talked to Ms. Ayana about once a week before she came. She was always cordial, so I didn't know if she really liked me or if she was fronting. But after everyone went to bed Thanksgiving night we stayed up talking. She actually thanked me for loving her son. I'm happy as shit that she's feeling me because Quinnzel's a mama's boy for real. It ain't about nothing though, I think it's sweet. Plus, any man who loves and respects his momma will love and respect his woman. Please believe me. Deal with a man who'll scream on his mom, trust that same nigga will knock your ass out.

The holiday season was a blur of folks, smiles, and good times. But I'm vexed y'all with KB Toy Stores selling pregnant Barbie dolls. What type of shit is that? All I'm a say is this; you mold the woman your daughter will become-what are you teaching her. Anyway before I knew it we counted down to 2003. A New Year slash my 26th birthday. Quinnzel and Dezionne threw me a blowout bash at the club and got Teena Marie live. I had a six tier birthday cake and crazy gifts from everybody. Ms. Ayana sent me two cruise tickets to the Caribbean and a picture she took of me and Q-daddy in an 8X10 Versace frame with the inscription '*Tender Love Don't Hate*'. That night Quinnzel lit fifty candles and presented me with a lavish pearl colored full-length chinchilla fur with a five-foot train and a yellow diamond watch.

Cheddar is definitely better.

I stayed at the office late Tuesday evening after Dezionne went to the rec. I'm focused reviewing post game conference tapes from last night's game against Indiana. I have noticed more efficient questions being asked regarding on-court recently. Leaving controversial personal lifestyles, which influence belittling perceptions and negative stereotypes, out of the public eye keeping the focus on basketball. Miracle Media magic, yup yup. I turned the tape off after Coach Larry Brown's interview. He gives me much support all day and I give him much love and mad props, especially for his induction into the Hall of Fame. I gathered my notes from the conference room and went in my office. I pulled the player portfolios from the file cabinet and sat at my desk to construct the monthly progress report. I buried myself in my work so depressing thoughts of my mom wouldn't wander. Her birthday is January 18th and I'm dreading our annual expedition to her gravesite. Daddy goes to see her twice a month but I have never been able to go to the cemetery by myself. Neither has Amir. Of course Quinnzel is coming with us, but his presence won't make the journey any less of a hardship.

Life for me ain't been no crystal stair without my right hand. In my little life, all my mom ever wanted for me was success. That's exactly why this year is the worst. Now that all of my dreams are coming true, I feel so betrayed that she's not here to bask in my glory. My falling tears soaked the pages in front of me. I let my tears of anguish fall recklessly, smearing letters and words together. I cried until my head started pounding. I dried my face, closed my eyes, and got myself together. The phone rang as I walked out of the office, so I let it roll over to the answering service. I dropped my briefcase and pocketbook when I heard Amir's estranged voice on the machine.

"Amir, I'm here. What up?"

"Daddy is in the hospital."

The tears I just cried for my mom resurfaced for my dad.

"What happened?"

"He fell while cooking out on the deck. I took him to the ER. They think he has diabetes."

"I'm on my way."

I flew to Abington Hospital and was greeted by our family doctor, Dr. Lewis Frank. He told me my dad's sugar count was up to eight hundred so he's actually lucky he collapsed when he did. Me and Amir went and sat with dad and I held his hand while he slept. I looked at my father; glad he's okay but upset with him for not taking better care of himself. But a bull-headed man doesn't believe shit stinks until he falls in it. Dr. Frank constantly tells my dad to cut back on greasy, sugary, fatty foods. And daddy constantly eats pizza, glazed doughnuts, cheese steaks, and fried chicken with no remorse. After today's episode I'll make for damn sure the nutrition label on everything he eats smacks him upside his head. I smiled and kissed my daddy when he finally opened his eyes. He apologized to me and Amir and hugged us as tight as he could with what little strength he had. Dad's friend, Mrs. Ilene, walked in a half an hour later with blankets and pillows. Seeing her come to support my dad made me realize I haven't called Q.

"I have plates from today's fish fry for you two in my car," she said propping a pillow under my dad's head.

Mrs. Ilene is a widowed schoolteacher. After twenty years of separation between them, she finally asked my dad to join her for dinner. I'm grateful to her for giving my Dad someone to care about besides Amir and me after ten years of loneliness.

"Thank you." I hugged Mrs. Ilene.

She gave her keys to Amir and we went outside to her car to eat. When we came back she elected herself to stay the night. I was about to argue her down until I looked at my father. He nodded his heavy head sealing his approval for her to stay. I guess her comfort would be more satisfying than mine. Me and Amir kissed Dad goodnight and I told him I would be back in the morning.

Amir followed me home and I parked my car. I jumped in his

pimped out Mustang and we headed to the Palace for some drinks. I went upstairs to the balcony and chilled in VIP. Amir hit the scene. After about twenty minutes Amir and Q walked over. Quinnzel had a gallon of E&J, a three-liter bottle of coke, and a bucket of ice. What more can a girl ask for? Quinnzel kissed me and I freaked him with my tongue until my wet panties chilled me. Yes, I am definitely satisfied. Amir had two drinks with us before he was ready to see a show.

"I'll holla top dollars," he said and gave Q a pound before he went downstairs.

I finished my third drink feeling nice.

"You chill?" my man asked me.

I looked at my chocolate dream.

"You know it."

"Round two?"

"Handle that." It's always round two with Q.

I reflected on our nine months of pleasure and pain. It's funny, my mommy used to say to folks when they would stress about my dad being at the stores all crazy, his love is pain because pain is love. I figured the same for my Quinnzel in between Cierra and the shootout. He fixed my drink and put his arm back around me. I peeped Dezionne coming up on the glass elevator. She gave me a pound and slapped Q upside his head big sister style. Amir knows about those. Dezionne sat in the love seat beside us.

"What's the deal peoples," she said sounding just like DeShawn.

I wonder if I sound like Quinnzel.

"Maintaining," Q said opening a Corona. "What it look like down there?"

"It's flowing," Dezionne said. She crossed her long legs. "Fix me a drink Quinn. What's popping Nae?"

"Same old shit just a different day." Yeah, I sound just like Quinnzel. "What's the business?"

"You know," she said sitting back with her glass. "I got that thing for you too Sis."

"Holla later."

She must've picked up the '02 Dodge Ram 1500 I got Q for his birthday February 14th. We celebrate our love everyday of the year, so I want Valentine's Day to be all about Quinnzel. Stan was coming upstairs on the elevator so Q got up to meet him.

"Excuse me babe," he said rubbing my neck.

"Don't trip," Dezionne said when Quinnzel walked away. "It's cool."

"It's cool." I sipped my E&J. "What's the ride looking like?"

"A silver bullet, baby sis."

I smiled.

"I love it."

I looked over at the window and saw Quinnzel whispering to Stan. I turned my head and glanced through the VIP crowd. I shitted when I saw Amir in the corner hugged up with Jovan.

Quinnzell Supreme Sharpe

Imani was bugging out when she saw Amir with Jovan a couple of weeks ago. I broke it down to her like; Amir is a thorough young bull let him do what he does. He may be your younger brother, but he's still a man. Plus, Jovan already know you can box. Imani analyzed my piece and was feeling me. We've been kicking it with her pops on the regular, talking shit, playing pinochle and monopoly. I stop by Mr. Darren's crib solo too. Imani doesn't know her pop is an original gangster retired. He used to run casinos in the back of his stores. That's why he spent so much time in them jawns, to clock shit.

The night after Imani, her peoples, and me came back from Raleigh North Carolina she and Dezionne went out west to Minnesota with the Sixers. My mind is on some jealousy shit with this stolen number that is still burning a hole in my two-way. Fuck this suspense shit, I switched the out-bound line and called that shit up. Some dude answered the horn all husky.

"Who the fuck is this?"

"Excuse me." Dude sounds like a buster.

"You called Imani, fool?"

"Listen dog," dude said clowning me. "I don't speak Ebonics, if you want to talk to me use your vowels."

"Dude I'll fuck you up." He laughed at me.

"Typical hip-hop thug."

"What, you Uncle Tom…" Dude got fired up.

"You illegitimate street peon," he said snapping. "You kill your own people and you call me an Uncle Tom. You're helping crackers make black men an endangered species stupid ass. I'm a real man; you're a fucking joke. You're beneath Imani. Matter of fact, tell her to call Derek when she's tired of dodging bullets."

Dude hung up on me and I lay in my bed fucked up in the head. I don't believe Imani's talking about me to this nigga. I tossed and turned all night because sleep is not an option. I know Imani's flight comes in at three in the a.m. I woke her ass up at five.

"Hey baby, did you miss me?"

"No. Who is Derek, Imani?"

"Baby, Derek is someone I dealt with before I met you."

She's trying to play me.

"So why is he still paging you?"

Her whole demeanor changed.

"You checked my two-way?" I didn't answer her.

"Why is dude talking about I'm killing my own people on the street and when you're tired of dodging bullets to call him because he's a real man. Like the fuck I'm not. Dude don't know me."

"Quinnzel, I don't talk to Derek. He said what he assumed," she said screaming at me. "You don't trust me enough to believe that?"

I ain't say shit.

"Huh, well don't be so insecure Quinnzel. You have never been Supreme to me, remember. Good night."

Imani hung up and I laid there feeling so sick. She has never hid shit from me she has no secrets. And I flipped on her over some shit this tight-ass nigga said. Damn. I want to call her back but my pride ain't let me show it. It's my fault too. I knew dude wouldn't say shit I wanted to hear. I'd been on some Tough Tony shit too if I was dude, yamean. Trust is a muthfucka. I expect Imani to trust me and endure all of my bullshit but I don't do the same for her. She never asked any questions, she just rode with me. Now, I'm all-alone on a one-way street. My silence feels like work so every minute salvaged my subconscious. An hour passed and I called Imani back. She didn't answer the phone and I don't want to leave a message. I hung up the phone and lay back on

my bed. I know she's going to work so I'll call her later. I nodded out around seven o'clock.

De woke me up at ten on some real drawing ass shit.

"What nigga?"

"Yo, get dressed. We got to make moves."

From the tone of his voice I know this ain't about any bullshit. I took a shower, got dressed, and went downstairs. De was
rolling a blunt out in the gazebo. I sat down and De took the lid
off of a dusty vertical gift-box that was sitting on the table. Four
long-stem roses, spray- painted black, covered in dirt was in that
shit.

"What the fuck?"

"This shit was on the door-step when I came home this morning," De said sparking a blunt. "I got to pick up two big ass
Uhaul's in a minute. We're going to take what we need and fuck
the rest of that shit."

I'm the fuck dazed.

"Niggas know where we rest our heads?"

"Not anymore," De said and he put his arm around my neck.
"Look baby boss, get your mind right. We got to handle shit."

I shook my head. When it rains niggas get the fuck wet. X,
you damn right.

"Supreme!!"

"What's up?"

"Call Amir and tell little nigga we need some help."

"Cool."

"That nigga wheeling?" De asked.

"Yeah."

"Bet. Tell him to meet you at the Palace, and then have his
freak move his car."

De passed me the blunt.

"Niggas ain't know we put the G in gangster," he said and
rolled out.

I sat there smoking, contemplating shit. Niggas who know
where you rest your head cause chaos. No matter how much hot

shit you hold, a nigga coming on the sneak got the upper hand. And even ice turns to water when it's hot. Look at Nino.

I called Amir and told him what was up. He said he'd meet me in a half. I rolled out and got to the club at eleven o' clock. Amir's Mustang was parked out front but he wasn't out there. I went inside to call his cell. I heard giggling and knocking as the stank of sweaty ass assaulted my nose. It ain't nobody but Jovan. Her ass has a key to the stage entrance she's only supposed to use to prep for concerts she opens for. I opened the door to the side-room and saw Amir with his pants at his ankles and Jovan's legs up around his neck. Her head was knocking against the floor to the beat of their stanktivity. That's why Jovan's so dizzy, banging her head against floors and shit. I flipped the light switch making the glow lights disappear.

"Cut that shit out."

"Oh shit," Amir said when he turned around and saw me. But my man damn sure didn't stop his stroke. "I'm coming in a minute."

I don't know if he's talking about coming outside or coming period.

"Hurry up and leave the way y'all came in."

I turned the light off and went back outside laughing my ass off. I waited in the Lamborghini about ten minutes before I saw them walking around the side. Jovan slobbed Amir down and young bull threw me the keys to the club.

"You must've known what it was, Jovan," I said and started the car.

She put her middle finger up and walked to Amir's car. He lifted the door up and got in. I waited for Jovan to pull off before we did.

Two white boys in a fucked up pick-up backed out of the driveway when I pulled up. I saw the Uhauls behind the crib so I figured one drove a truck up here and the other came with for security, yamean. They don't get down with us like that, whitey only fuck with us to get money. De was sitting in the gazebo

with four blunts rolled and two large-ass pizzas on the table. I
don't believe I'm smoking all crazy now. But weed actually be
helping me focus. We grubbed, smoked two blunts, and got that
shit in. We moved the beds, electronics, all of the furniture, and
tossed our gear in the back of the Ford. De arranged for all of the
utilities to be shut off tomorrow. We blazed up and rolled out
about five o' clock.

De drove the Ford while me Amir followed in the Uhaul's.
I'm coming back for my fly ass Lamborghini, fuck the rest of
those wheels. I'll cop some fresh shit tomorrow, yamean. Money
ain't a thang. See, you know you're on the top of the game when
you can make any move when deemed necessary. Real niggas do
real things you know. Hustlers with potential got to flip one more
brick before they can motivate. Fake ass thugs wasting time, taking up space got to wait until they re-up four or five more times
before they can ride out majorly or otherwise. Those nickel and
dime cats fuck the block up for real niggas pushing weight.
Know your role. You stay on top by being smarter and sharper
than the next nigga. Your Presidents have to stay big and run
long yamean. And yo, don't mistake this move right here to be on
no running scared shit. You have to maintain your home front at
all costs. Your crib has to be your safe haven from the street. All
rah-rah shit and drama is made for the block. If niggas violate
and bring beef to your spot, that's their ass. It's about protecting
your neck while glazing niggas necks. Please believe we're going
to find out who made the surprise delivery and those cats are
ghosts. Speaking of shifty niggas on some grimy shit, I ain't tell
De about the drama Stan kicked at me. I definitely got to holla at
my ace on this one.

We pulled up to a dual crib at the top of a block shaped like a
horseshoe. Mad kids were outside running around throwing
snowballs, making snow angels. Chimney's smoking, dads shov-
eling. We done landed in the middle of a fucking Leave-it-to-
Beaver episode. Only difference, siddity ass black folks populate
this section of Fredricks, Maryland. Shit, I already counted four

yachts and three golf courses. Get the fuck out of here with that
yachting shit. That ain't no sport it's pimping leisurely. We
parked the Uhauls in the garage and De threw me a set of keys. I
peeped the outside set up. Kidney shaped pools, Jacuzzi in the
cuts, arena- sized basketball court. That's what's up. I ain't run
rock in a nice minute. Now I can bust De's ass on the regular. I
walked through the old-fashioned wooden built patio into the
kitchen. Damn this crib is ghetto fabulous. I can definitely chill
here. I went upstairs to check out the rooms. Every one is hitting
for something. I ran down the back steps and De was on the
landing.

"What the fuck, how you get in here?"

"Nigga the cribs are connected by the back stairs."

"I'm a have to remember that."

"True. Let's be out."

De locked the garage up and we rolled in the F150 back to
Jersey. I got in my wheel and Amir rolled with me back to the
Palace. We got to the office like one in the muthafucking morning. Dezionne took Amir to his crib so me and De could bust it
up.

"Yo Money, we got heat coming at us like missiles."

"Who's the next victim to fall," De said splitting a green
Dutch.

"Nigga's talking about joining forces to battle us on some
WWIII shit."

De looked at me.

"Who?"

"Blalock and that faggot ass Joey."

"Damn niggas hate when you getting money like athletes,"
De said sparking up. "Jigga you ain't ever lied. Shit. Call a meeting."

Imani

I'm worried. Quinnzel's number at home is disconnected and I haven't heard from him in a minute. I know he's upset about Derek, but I should be the one feeling some type of way. I never check his two-way no matter how many times the bitch goes off all types of the night. Shit. Unconditional love is about trust, honesty, commitment, compromise and sacrifice but it can never be a one-way street. Damn. Quinnzel means the world to me and I feel it inside that he is my survivor. I have to let him know he's in violation, it's only right. We all make mistakes and I'm ready to forgive my man so we can move on. I'm missing his carnal ass like crazy. But they say absence makes the heart grow fonder. And I say that after an argument the lovemaking is incredible. Damn, I got to have that man. Woo. I'm getting chills just thinking about it. I'm not going to page him because I don't want to be rekindled digitally. I wish I knew where he lived so I could conduct a freakcapde of my own. I guess I have to wait for him to call me. I just pray he's not going through anything too drastic.

On a brighter note, tomorrow is the first shoot for my introductory commercial. They're profiling the interaction of Miracle Media and the NBA, using Sixers' highlights. I share the responsibility of selecting electrifying slams, assists, and commentary for the commercial. I'm magnetically attracted to the announcers' remarks because of their exuberant reactions. From Mark and Steve to Marv and Mike to the cast of Inside the NBA their voices seize the bomb plays. I definitely welcome the challenge.

Snowflakes fell softly outside of my bedroom window late Sunday evening. I got up to pop some popcorn and put Love Jones in the DVD player. I love Nia Long she is so beautiful. Just as I pulled the covers over me the phone rang.

"Yes."

"Imani," the voice stuttered.

"Who is this?" There was a brief pause.

"Derek," he said breathing heavily. It sounds like he's drinking.

"What's up Derek?" I don't feel like dealing with him right now.

"You're wrong Imani," he said stammering. "I could have given you the world but you turned your back on me for a thug-ass, ruff neck, drug pusher."

"Derek I don't owe you an explanation," I said and paused my movie. "As a matter of fact I don't owe you anything."

There was an awkward silence between us. Derek is searching for something that was never there.

"Imani I need you."

"Derek you are drunk and you're tripping. Please do not call me again. Take care of yourself."

"Bitch I'll…"

I hung up the phone and it rang right back.

"Imani I don't know what came over me," Derek said giggling. "Please forgive me."

This fool is pissy drunk.

"I forgive you. Now please Derek, leave me be."

"I won't let you leave me Imani."

"Good-bye Derek. That means forever."

I hung up the phone and sat back on my bed. Fuck is wrong with dude?

I pressed play on my DVD remote. Hello Morning. I fell asleep watching the movie and woke up around eleven o' clock. I'm hungry but I need to go shopping. I threw on some thermals and sweats and drove up to PathMark. Crisp winter air whipped through my leather coat as I ran into the store on Wayne and Chelten. It's not crowded so I got a front parking space and shopped for an hour. I love shopping at night. I loaded my groceries in my trunk and pushed the cart back to the rack. I walked back to my car and heard footsteps creeping behind me. I turned around and saw Derek approaching me. I reached for my pepper-spray but it's in my pocketbook, in the car. Fuck. I ran to my car and he chased me. I pressed the button on my alarm unlocking my doors. Derek lunged at me knocking me to the ground. He sat on top of me and smashed my face in the snow. Derek wrapped my ponytail around his gloved hand and turned me over. He pulled a raven from his coat-pocket and cocked it against my head. A bitch-ass gun for a bitch-ass nigga. He ran the barrel from my temple down the side of my face and put it in my mouth.

"You like it ruff right Imani." Derek reeked of Old Spice and Southern Comfort. "Stand up," he shouted.

I stood up shivering from cold and fear. This nigga is ill.

"Walk." Derek put the gun under my coat and aimed it at my spine.

We walked across the street and he led me to a darkened corner in Picket Junior High School parking lot. My tears froze on my cheeks. Derek took his arm from around me and aimed the gun at my head.

"Lay down."

I did what he said and didn't say a word. Derek pulled his pants down and his tiny dick was already hard. He pulled my bottoms off and got on top of me. I closed my eyes and turned my head. I cried. Derek forced my legs open and thrust himself inside of me. He humped like a wounded dog for five minutes before he came. He pulled out and pumped his nut on my cheek.

"Was that ruff enough for you bitch," he said rubbing his semen over my face. "Who's the man now Imani. I got the power."

He stood and took off running with his pants dangling around his ankles. I lay there motionless until he disappeared. I turned over and threw up until there was nothing left inside of me. I hobbled back to my car and flew to Dezionne's house like a bat out of hell.

"Oh my God," Dezionne said when I crawled in her door. "Imani what happened?"

Tears formed in her eyes before I opened my mouth. She called the police and an ambulance after I told her about Derek's trifling ass.

Dezionne made me a cup of chamomile tea and wrapped a quilt around my bleak body. She held me like a nurturing mother until blazing lights and flaring sirens filled the block. I was rushed to Abington Hospital. Traces of Derek's semen were recovered from my vaginal area and face and the doctor performed a rape kit. I was finally able to shower after Dr. Maxwell concluded his tests and screening for evidence. He also gave me antibacterial cream for my face. I turned the water temperature on hell and scrubbed with a vengeance. I gave my statement to Detective Howard and Dr. Maxwell told me I have to stay for a few days for follow-up and additional testing. I lay in the hospital bed with Dezionne at my side.

"Ms. Best it is common for rapist to attack people they know," Detective Howard said before he left.

I guess those were supposed to be words of comfort. Dezionne held my hand and rubbed my head. She beared the weight of my tragedy and suffered with me.

"Thank you Dezionne."

"Hush sweetie. You do what you have to do for family."

I hugged Dezionne and we cried together. This shit clogged in my mind. Raping me actually made Derek feel like he accomplished something meaningful. I would never have imagined he could emulate such hatred for me as much as he prides himself on preserving black women. Beyond that, after the tragic summer of our Children of Peril, a father of two beautiful girls actually had the gall to rape someone's daughter. Our fallen angels deserve more from us.

Devastated Monday morning, Dezionne called Drake and told him we had to postpone the shoot. I asked her not to call my Dad until I had strength enough for both of us to keep level heads. Derek's bloody massacre would have been breaking news if daddy would've seen me last night. Shit yeah Derek is going to suffer hellified consequences, but I don't need my dad in jail too. It's obvious Derek didn't think about tomorrow when he made the decision to gamble with my life. Damn, I really need the comfort of my man.

"Did Q call, pass me my two-way."

Dezionne smiled and stood up. She pulled the partitioned drapes apart and Quinnzel stood up like an island of lost dreams surrounded by my sea of disarray. He smiled revealing those enchanting dimples, melting my despair. Quinnzel came to me.

"I promise to keep you safe forever." He delicately kissed my forehead. "Even if I have to die for you."

I wiped his tears and joyously hugged him as tight as I could.

"You aight?" Quinnzel asked holding me. "I'm a take care of you."

His reassuring words of endearment warmed my aching mind. I value his culminating devotion. Quinnzel is my hero.

"Dog I'm feeling the shit out of you," I said kissing him. We laughed together.

"It's a Kodak moment," Dezionne said sitting back on her chair.

I don't know how or when she got Quinnzel here, but I love her for it. Dezionne is an ill sister. I admire her spunk. She handles business neatly; she's compassionate and generous. It's not too many sisters on her level now a days. I'm grateful to have her by my side. Quinnzel stood up and went to the window. I know him well enough to know he's contemplating revenge. And I'm not sure I want to stop him, but I don't need Quinnzel in jail either.

"Imani, do you need anything?" Quinnzel said walking back over to me.

He must've known I was thinking about him.

"Apple-cranberry juice," I said and smiled like the Gerber baby.

"I'll be back in ten minutes." Quinnzel grabbed his coat. "Dez, you cool?"

"Nah brother, I need some breakfast."

"Damn who I look like Mrs. Butterworth," Quinnzel said laughing. "Yo, for real I could roll down to Bilal's."

"That's what's up," Dezionne said snapping her fingers. "I want a fish and grits platter nigga. And you better fly in your space shuttle on wheels."

"Oh you clowning my whip?"

"Nah baby boss you got the dope ride." Dezionne gave Quinnzel a pound. "That shit is the hottest."

I love watching them; they have so much fun together. Quinnzel put his coat on and smacked Dezionne with his coat tail.

"My bad," he said laughing. "Imani, what do you want to eat?"

"You know what I like baby, surprise me." I winked at Quinnzel.

He blew me a kiss and walked out of the door. I looked at Dezionne.

"What's his plan?"

Dezionne closed her eyes and shook her head.

"Dezionne?"

"Imani think. Is Quinnzel really going to let this ride?"

"I am so sick of this wanksta shit," I said holding back my tears. "Supreme may be a master of disguise but he is not God."

Dezionne got up from her chair and sat beside me.

"Imani listen." Her tone was quiet. "Supreme is not the man you fell in love with, Quinnzel is, and he is a man; a provider, protector. And in his mind it's an eye for an eye."

"Dezionne, foremost in my mind is keeping Quinnzel safe and out of trouble."

Before she could say anything the door flew open and my Dad ran to my bedside. Quinnzel must have called him.

"Him too," I said hugging my father.

Dezionne laughed and rubbed my head. She stood up and excused herself.

"Nae Nae, are you okay?"

"Yes daddy, I'm fine."

"When I find that son-of-a-bitch…"

"Daddy no. Please. I don't need you in jail for killing nobody."

"Baby girl listen…"

"No, you listen," I said calmly. "We have to think carefully when wrong is upon us. Remember. You taught me that."

Dad wiped his tears and stood up. He went to the same window Quinnzel did. After about ten minutes Dad laughed heartily and clapped his hands.

"You're right Nae Nae," Dad said turning around to face me. "I'm proud of you. But I bet you need some help getting Quinnzel to swallow that pill."

I wiped my tears and looked intently into my dad's eyes. This is scary!

Quinnzell Supreme Sharpe

The cops caught Derek's mark ass lecturing his first period class Monday morning. He actually took his Professor Peabody ass to work like it wasn't shit. He's lucky 5-0 got his ass before I did. I ain't even call Blaze. I was going to off that nigga myself. I felt that shit. That's all I have to say about that nigga.

The whole fam went to see the Sixers play Orlando on my birthday. Imani gave me a shot-out on the big screen before tip-off. At halftime she took me outside and gave me the keys to a sweet ass Dodge Ram already chromed out on some big phat wheels. I was out there girling and shit, jumping up and down screaming, "Oh my God." I knew she spent a grip when I opened the glove box and saw the tags, title, registration, and insurance card. I don't have to do shit but drive. Imani had dinner waiting for us at Mr. Darren's crib after the game too. My lady went all out.

Saturday, I rolled to the block to collect. I was in and out of the crib in fifteen minutes and I stashed the loot in my ride. De pulled up behind me before I pulled off. He walked up to my truck and got in.

"What's the deal Money?" De gave me a pound.

"Shit is getting wicked baby boss. Let's ride."

De got out and got in his whip. He followed me to the Palace.

"What's going on," I said sitting down with a Corona and a blunt.

"Rahiem hipped me to some shit," De said as he sparked his blunt. "Thomas and Williams is trying to stick us to some missing persons shit."

"Who the fuck is missing?"

"Nino and his bitch ass crew."

"Damn."

"It's cool dude check it," De said. "They ain't got no evidence. They just know he rode with us."

"Bet," I said smoking. "We just tell them Nino told us he was going out of town…"

"And that's all we know," De said finishing my sentence. "It's like butter baby."

I gave De a pound and we laughed like shit.

"What's the verdict on Joey and Blalock?"

"The jury's still out," De said opening a Corona. "But I got niggas clocking their blocks all day. If they break out on a mission, we'll know before they ante up."

"Cool."

"We'll holla at 5-0 tomorrow and clean this Nino shit up."

"Word. We don't need them niggas creeping."

"Oh shit," De said jumping up. "Let me tell you how it was those pussies that put the flowers on the step."

"Get the fuck out of here nigga."

"Yo I ain't bullshitting cousin," De said laughing his ass off. "Yeah, Rahiem heard those niggas talking in the locker room and shit. They looked like dickheads when they came back swat deep with a warrant."

"Damn is it cool though?"

"After we bust it up with them. They ain't got shit as it is. I'll make sure they leave us the fuck alone."

De gave me a pound and we laid back getting fucked up.

Thoughts of Imani invaded my get high. Damn. We ain't got that shit in since the rape. I mean I hold her all night but I be feeling some type of way and shit. Like I see that nigga on top of my girl with a gun at her dome and she's crying and shit. My blood starts boiling and I be sweating all crazy. I can't sex my lady with psychotic thoughts crashing my brain. I don't even know if Imani wants to make love. She'll wrap her legs around me and rub my back but we always wind up bussing it up or just going to sleep. It ain't about shit though; I respect her feelings all day. I just don't know how to come at her. It ain't really shit I can say to her to quiet those thoughts or feelings she has. I mean rape is a fucked up experience that no woman should have to encounter. Imani ain't want to go to therapy to rap about it and clear her dome. So right now I'm maintaining Imani's happiness. No matter what's going down, when she gets off work I'm there. We're eating at all places, shooting pool at Jillian's, getting drinks, it doesn't matter. We're riding where ever. I take Imani home; we chill, play cards, chess, whatever. And if I have to roll I don't leave until after she's asleep. But I'm always back before she wakes up. Fuck that. I need to be the last person she sees before she goes to sleep and the first person she sees when she wakes up. I have to, for Imani's sake and my piece of mind. I called Imani at work.

"Good Afternoon, thank you for calling Miracle Media week-end edition. This is Dezionne Sinclair how may I assist you?"

"You sound all country and shit," I said mocking Dez. She laughed. "Nah for real sis, what's the deal?"

"Cooling."

"Where wifey at?"

"Hold on."

"Good Afternoon," Imani said sounding sexy as shit. "This is Imani H. Best how may I assist you?"

"Can you make it last forever?"

"That's my word." I smiled.

"Word is bond?"

"All day." We laughed together.

"What's popping tonight?"

"We are." She fucked my head up with that one.

"Imani"

"Hush baby," Imani said. I feel her smiling. "I got this."

"Damn gangster."

Imani blew a kiss through the receiver. That shit hit me like KABOOM. Damn.

"I'm in love with you, girl."

"I'm in love with you shorty rock."

"Jillian's tonight?"

"Let's do the damn thing."

"Holla. So long beautiful."

"Later baby."

I hung up the phone smiling my ass off.

"Your bosom sure knows how to brighten your fucking day," De said looking at me.

"You damn skippy."

I chilled at the office with De until four. I got a freshy boy haircut and stopped at Imani's crib to switch my gear up. I took a shower and threw on tan Dickies, a sorrel Polo sweater, and butter timbs. I zipped up my butter leather and rolled out. Imani walked through the glass doors when she saw the Lamborghini roll up at six. I got out and lifted the door up. Imani kissed me so tender she made my dick wet.

"Let's go home," Imani said before she got in the car.

You only have to tell me one time.

I jumped in the whip and rolled back to Imani's spot. She freaked me from the elevator to the door. The wait's over. I locked the front door behind us. Now I'm here like I've been before. I ran a bubble bath for Imani and washed her entire body. I massaged her feet and sucked her toes. Imani stood up in the water and took my clothes off. We sat down and I rested between her thighs. She ran her hands down my chest and palmed my dick. He stood up with one stroke of her hand.

"Come on," Imani whispered in my ear.

We got out of the tub and I followed Imani to the bedroom. I laid her down and oiled her body. Imani stung me with her sweet kiss. I nibbled her titties like they were peaches, my muthfucking favorite. I explored my taffy and sent Imani to new unabated heights of orgasms. She came four times before my love muscle did any work. I eats that shit up right, yamean. I looked up at Imani and she had her eyes closed, biting her bottom lip, squeezing pillows and shit. She looks pretty as shit when she's coming. Damn. Imani got on top of me and sat down on my dick. I moaned with each wind of her sugary hips. "Heaven must be missing an angel tonight." I joked.

"Imani," I said smacking her ass. "Imani, Imani, damn baby."

She leaned down on me and bit my ear. I flipped Imani over and gave her the entire dick.

"I love you Imani," I said feeling her come.

Imani kissed me and held me as tight as she could. I rubbed her back and kissed her shoulder. I blew out the candles and we lay down. I wrapped my arm around Imani and she held my hand.

"I love you too Quinnzel," she moaned as she kissed my hand.

I'm a sleep good tonight. I nodded out and my two-way woke me up on a three piece. It's not De. I don't know whose number this is. Imani walked out of the bathroom and saw me checking my pager.

"You have to go," she said getting back in the bed. She kissed my neck.

"Nah beautiful, go back to sleep."

"That's not DeShawn."

"I don't know the number."

"Convenient."

I know where this is going.

"Imani do you want to call the number back?"

"No Quinnzel. Good night."

Imani pulled the covers up over her shoulders. I'm not having this shit. I pulled the covers off of her.

"Aside from you this pager is for business," I said before Imani could say anything. "I want you to block your number, call the number back, and ask did somebody call Supreme."

Imani frowned her face when I said Supreme.

"Alright then, don't fuck with Supreme shit."

"Give me the phone," Imani said rolling her eyes at me.

She snatched the phone from me and mumbled something.

"Don't pussy foot around your words, speak up Cannon."

Imani stood up and hit me with a pillow.

"I said punk-ass."

I threw her on the bed and tickled my baby all crazy. She damn near choked from laughing. I kissed Imani and laid down.

"So what's up?" She threw the phone on the bed.

"I trust you Quinnzel, it's business."

"That's what's up," I said picking up the phone. "I still want to know who this is; you might as well call back. Just do what I said."

Imani picked up my two-way and dialed the number.

"Yeah you page Supreme." Imani tried to sound tough as shit. My gangster boogie.

"And who is this?" She got loud. "Who the fuck is Tasha?"

"Tasha?" I scratched my head.

Shit, the only Tasha I know is Nino's baby mom. I took the phone from Imani.

"Who the fuck is this?"

"Yeah bitch you know who the fuck this is."

I played the dummy role.

"Oh shit. What's up Tasha? Where that nigga Nino been at?"

She started screaming me.

"Nigga YOU know where the fuck Nino is, ain't nobody seen him for months," Tasha said sniffling. "Where is he?"

Damn I know her ass told 5-0 whatever it is she's implying now.

"Yo, I don't know shorty but you got to holla back," I said looking at Imani. "I'm with my wifey right now."

"Supreme…"

"Later Tasha. One."

I hung up the phone and put it on the charger. No telling if she got her phone tapped or not. The cops could've been listening to that whole shit. I know Imani heard Tasha but of course she ain't say shit. Imani just turned off the light. I wondered who else she called.

Imani

Love is an idle emotion often hidden in the life of a thug nigga. He can't be rattled by that weak shit on the block, oh no. But when he experiences an authentic woman who stimulates, satisfies, and tames all levels of his being that thug nigga will submit. In the same token, thug niggas live in a war. Quinnzel is a prisoner of both worlds and I'm lost by his side dealing with our love and his war. Our love is quiet amidst his battle of bull-shit. I can't fight with him. Quinnzel asked me to share his world but thug nigga Supreme isn't ready to receive me. I can't help but to wonder if he killed Nino. The urgency in Tasha's voice was shrilling. And Dezionne did say it was Nino who Q banged guns with at the club. Damn, I need to holla at Mrs. Cleo. The phone rang breaking my concentration.

"Hello."

"Hello Imani."

"And who is this?" I didn't recognize the voice.

"This is Jovan."

"Oh."

At first I thought Amir's masquerade with Jovan was a nasty sexcapade. But they've been dealing for a couple of months and my baby brother's happy.

"Imani?"

"I'm here, speak." I still don't like the bitch.

"Damn, I'm trying to be polite."

"And I'm trying to be forward. There's no need for small talk, spit it the fuck out."

"Never mind Imani. I thought you were a grown-ass woman."

"I'm your idol's icon sweetie. Check my resume."

Jovan hung up like I give a fuck.

I sat reviewing the files I brought home with me. I'm concentrating on the NC2A with March Madness upon us. And the end of the regular season ends my season with the pros. The draft is my next big move. I'm hooking up a party for the Sixers, before the play-offs, for showing me nothing but love all year. I orchestrated a coalition of AI supporters to get his name on the 2004 Olympic team roster. This is a sensitive subject for me because I have to remain unbiased, but the fact is throughout his illustrious seven-year career in the NBA, AI more than validated his talents and proved he deserves the opportunity to represent the United States in the tournament. If he doesn't, who does?

AI changes the whole dynamic of the game. He is one of the best one on one guards ever, he can take anybody off the dribble, and he's a beast in the open court. Nobody can guard him man up, his jab step is the best in the business, his crossover breaks defenders ankles worldwide, and defenses collapse on him instantly when he drives {he's damn near triple teamed whenever he touches the ball} so he can penetrate and dish at will. Which makes any team better because perimeter shooters will get wide open looks all night. AI I got your back, but like you said it ain't got anything to do with basketball. Day two of my commercial shoot is tomorrow. Yeah Yeah. I was finally able to summon the courage to go back to the moment when I was shoved off track. The commercial debuts on March 14th during the Sixers' game when the squad plays Portland celebrating the twenty-year mark of the 'un-fo-fo-fo-gettable' championship season.

Quinnzel called and told me he's going to be late. He's taking me to his new spot out in Maryland and I don't have to wear a blindfold. I'm breaking him down, but only Quinnzel can quit Supreme. I came to the indisputable truth that a woman can not change anything about a man that he is not ready to change nor wants to change. I don't want Q to resent me for bitching about something he was long before we were. Especially because his thug nature was what appealed to me. His rough exterior, his presence demands respect, his mind stays strong. He could have been so much more but Q and DeShawn's household of turmoil forced them to the mercy of the streets early on. Too many of our young brothers fall prey to the block because of misguidance, or lack thereof. They're not to blame. Fathers are things you hear about but don't see in the 'hood. I accept Quinnzel, and I'll make Supreme an inner struggle. He'll retire from street life in his own time. My love won't change. At six o' clock, I packed my bag and took a bath. I threw on a denim RocaWear outfit and my cinnamon suede timbs. I stomp shitty with the timb boots, please believe me. I combed out my wrap and bumped my edges. Damn, it's time to hit Malakia up to toss my shit. My stylist hooks my du up early. I heard my front door open. Quinnzel came in carrying a big brown bag. I followed him to the kitchen.

"What's up, baby?" Quinnzel kissed me and put the bag on the table.

I licked my lips.

"Hey baby, what's in the bag?"

"Fish fried rice."

"Bilal's?"

"Who else," Quinnzel said laughing at me. "Hello."

"You clowning me baby?"

We laughed our way into freak mode. We were about to get that shit in and the fucking phone rang. Who the fuck is it? I ignored the call until Amir started calling my name on the machine.

"Q, grab the phone babe," I said pushing him up. "Damn little brother."

"Yo...I'm cool what's up with you...Bet, let me know...Hold on."

Quinnzel passed me the phone and went for the food.

"What up peoples?"

"Why you got to dis my shorty?"

"Amir you sleep with Jovan, not me."

"And you fuck Q, but I still holla at the Bull," Amir said. "Damn Nae."

"Amir what do you want from me," I said walking into the living room. "Q never tried to get you strolled."

"That shit is old Nae come on. You beat her ass, she knows you ain't to be flexed with, move the fuck on.

I sat on the couch.

"Imani listen. I dig Jovan and I'm chilling with her. I'm asking you to squash that shit."

"Oh and you're content being rent-a-pop."

I shouldn't have said that.

"You know opinions are like assholes everybody has one. But feel me on this, holla at me when your man's eating a ten to twenty bid. One."

Amir banged on me. I hung up and called him right back. He didn't answer. I called my dad's crib and got no answer there. He's probably at Jovan's cave. She has her vampire claws dug in and she is devouring Amir's pockets. Shit. His smart-ass just graduated early from MIT. He said fuck the aisle, scooped up his degree, and linked up with Ford designing all model vehicles. My baby boy got crazy cash bonuses and incentives from Front Street. Quinnzel walked in the living room wiping his mouth.

"Are you going to eat? We have to roll in a minute."

I shook my head.

"Babe, my mouth just brought me something my ass can't afford."

"What's going on?" Quinnzel sat next to me on the couch.

"Me and Amir went through it over Jovan."

"Imani, what did I tell you about that?"

"So what am I supposed to watch her play my brother?"

"No," Quinnzel said turning my face towards him. "What you're not supposed to do is pass judgment. You're supposed to be supportive and play your part. When it's needed, then handle shit big sister."

Damn that makes absolute sense.

"Babe, what are you a philosopher now?"

Quinnzel kissed me and smiled.

"I'm whatever you need me to be. Let's be out."

Dry ice in the sink with hot water equals steam y'all, remember that. I lay trembling in Quinnzel's arms after our good loving. Our sweaty bodies shimmered under the dim lights. I want to stay like this forever. This is my rightful place. I slept melodious in our peaceful night. Quinnzel woke me up with his crazy love.

"Good Morning," he said kissing my forehead.

"It's a hellava morning now."

We laughed. Quinnzel got up and walked to his dresser. Damn. Zeus ain't got shit on my baby.

"Swing daddy."

"Sure you right."

Quinnzel laughed and put on his boxers. He brought my robe over to me. A peach, silky secret he gave me last night. Quinnzel kissed me and went in the bathroom. He ran my bath water and went downstairs. I stepped down into an herbal- passion bubble bath in Quinnzel's whirlpool tub. I turned on the massager and laid my head back. I closed my eyes and opened them to see Quinnzel standing over me. He bit his bottom lip and smiled. I grabbed his hand and pulled him in tub with me.

"Hold up babe, I'm cooking."

I smothered Quinnzel with kisses before I let him up. He pulled off his dripping boxers and wrapped a towel around his waist.

"I'll be back to wash you down."

"Holla."

Quinnzel disappeared just as the phone rang.

"Hello."

"Amir, what up?"

"What's the deal Imani?"

"Yo, A listen." I got up and went in the hallway. "As long as you're with Jovan, I don't have any beef."

"Good looking Nae. My bad for…"

"No apologies necessary okay baby boy."

"Imani, I'm good okay. I can handle Jovan, it ain't no thing.

Please believe me."

"Yeah, okay...just watch yourself."

I hung up the phone and went back in the bedroom. Quinnzel brought me breakfast, but we never got a chance to eat. Yeah, I fucked his ass to sleep for real. I give myself props for throwing that shit back early. I put the phone on the charger and got in the bed. I curled up beside my sleeping jewel.

Quinnzell Supreme Sharpe

"Those muthfuckas blew Dez crib up."

"Say what?"

"Where the fuck you been?"

De just bust in the office screaming some wild shit.

"I've been here."

"Not today nigga," De said stepping to me. "Niggas have been paging you all weekend. What the fuck is up Supreme?"

I don't have shit to say. I make no excuses.

"I was chilling with Imani."

"Chilling ain't handling business," De said with an ill grizzly. "You are your brothers' keeper, or did you forget?"

"You done," I said stepping back.

I sat on the couch and shook my head. Damn, this is fucked up.

"Look baby boss, I know you're loving it up with wifey and that's cool," De said sitting next to me. "But we have to maintain business and right now shit is not promising."

"You don't think I know that?"

"I know you know that shit," De said standing up. "Because we're about to go to war and Quinnzel can't be holding his skirt, bitching on the sideline."

"Nigga what?"

I jumped up and stood toe to toe with DeShawn. My fists balled up by they damn selves. But I deemed myself before it was too late.

"Shawn you're working with a lot of emotions. And I feel you. But we don't have to take it there."

I put my hand out to give De a pound. He just looked at me.

"Get your mind right Supreme. We have a meeting at eleven o' clock, or do you have to ask wifey?"

I put my hand down and looked in my brother's face.

"I'm saying what is this coming to?" De shook his head.

"Dez is at Imani's. I'm out."

He stepped back and walked out of the door. This shit is the worst.

Me and my brother never went through it over a female. And his beef is not Imani; it's me regarding Imani. I flipped the script and forgot I was a G. Fuck that. The Bull ain't going out like that. I locked up the office and rolled to Imani's. Double De was leaving when I pulled up. It's cool; I'll holla at De later. I know what it is. I parked and went inside. I smelled Imani's banging-ass spaghetti from the door. Turkey Italian sausage, ground beef, beef smoked sausage. She hooks that shit up with onions, mushrooms, red and green peppers, all types of spices and the sauce be kicking like Jackie Chan. But I don't want to eat. I ain't even say shit when I opened the door. I sat on the couch with my coat on like an unwelcomed guest. Imani ain't even hear me with dangerously in love on blast. She got the lights all dim and candles lit. I'm not feeling this right now. I got up to get out. Imani heard me open the door and came in the living room.

"What's up babe?"

"Cooling. What's up with you?"

"I'm good." Imani smiled at me. "Are you leaving?"

"Why you ask me that?"

"Because you're standing in the doorway."

"So?" I closed the door and sat on the couch.

"Q, what's up?" Imani kneeled in front of me.

"Nothing, watch out." I brushed her aside and she stood up.

"What is the problem?"

I feel Imani's eyes burning holes through me, but I didn't look at her. I stood up and went to the door.

"Quinnzel?"

Imani's desperate tone stopped me. I put my hand on the

doorknob and turned around with my head down.

"It's not working out."

"Not working out?"

I shook my head and opened the door.

"You can't look me in my eyes, Quinnzel?"

Imani pleaded with much hurt in her voice. I stepped in the hallway with my back to her.

"Good-bye Imani."

I closed the door and heard my heart break.

I drove around without a destination. A Range full of chickens pulled up beside me. They broke their necks trying to holla.

"Fuck broads," I said and pulled off.

Fuck them broads. I ain't digging up on nobody. It's going to be hard enough getting Imani out of my dome. I can't trip off of her no more. I got to handle business the way I'm suppose to. One shorty ain't fucking up my legacy. I hit niggas up and told them to go shut Tasha the fuck up. Nah, we don't kill no women or no kids, but we let everybody know it ain't a fucking game. I paged De and told him to meet me at O'Hara's in forty-five. I posted up at our table with my drink. I peeped this nigga in a bucket hat grilling me and shit. Dude stepped to me. I stood up with my hand on my nine.

"Supreme what the deal killer." Dude pulled his hat up and let his grill show.

"Oh shit, Malik."

I ran with Malik back in the day. He grew up on the block with us. We went to Georgetown together but he went over seas to run ball because he didn't get drafted.

"What's up nigga?" I gave Malik a pound and we sat down.

"I'm early in the game, what's up with you?"

"Maintaining. You know I don't do much."

"Let you tell it. Shit. Nigga you are a celebrity around these parts."

"What you talking about?"

"Nigga stop fronting. You and Money got this shit on lock

with fools hating from a distance."

Malik called the waitress over and ordered a bottle of Crown Royal.

"So what's good with you 'Lik."

"I'm here now trying to get scouted. My agent is putting me down with some Miracle Media shit for props."

Damn, Imani.

"But uh, I'm on a paper chase now. What's up?"

I ain't even hear him.

"Supreme?"

"What's up?"

"I'm trying to get money with y'all niggas."

"Let me holla at my peoples, we ain't ever got enough soldiers."

Malik gave me a pound. I picked up my glass and downed my drink. Shit, Imani's voice pounded in my head. I hear her call my name and it pierces me deep as the abyss.

"What's up with your peoples," I said.

"Everybody straight. Munchie got knocked."

"What?"

"I thought you knew, your mans was with him."

"Who?"

"Egg-head bull. What's his name?"

"Stan?"

"Yeah. They got hemmed up hitting a bank."

"Get the fuck out of here. When?"

What the fuck is Stan doing riding out with Munchie? Everybody knows he on that shit. Damn. You have to be a leader dog.

"Friday nigga damn, ain't these your streets."

Damn I was definitely out of commission laid up with Imani all crazy.

"Nigga you need some new eyes and ears, no doubt."

"Give me a number." Malik gave me a card.

"I'm meeting with this media chick at the end of the week.

Hit me up early."

"I got you."

"I'm out." Malik stood up and gave me a pound.

"Be safe playa. One."

I sat there on the solo with my mind flooded. Tasha's cosigning the federales; Dez crib got hit, Stan is caught up. Shit is thick.

"Baby boss," De pulled his chair out and sat down. "What's up my nigga?"

"Stan…"

"I know about Stan. He's not running his mouth yet. Let his stupid ass sit a while, we'll see."

"And Tasha already got us out there."

"Nino's Tasha?"

"Yup. She paged me talking about she know I know where he is."

"Shit I know she told 5-0 that same shit."

"True. True."

De lit a cigarette.

"Yo Money, I know where you was coming from and I feel you."

"It's serious now 'Preme. You can't be bullshitting."

"I'm with you all day, no question."

De stood up and put his hand out. I put my hand out and De pulled me out of my seat. My brother hugged me and our weight lifted.

"I got nothing but love for you Q for real." De kissed my cheek. "You're my man fifty grand. And you know Imani is my girl and a bag of pearls."

I sat back down and took my drink to the head. I ain't say shit about Imani. I have to deal with those ghosts on my own.

Imani

Nigga's will fuck your whole shit up. Just one month before our anniversary Quinnzel reneged on his commitment. He shattered my foundation. All of the lovey dovey bullshit in the previous eleven months was bullshit. I gave this man my all and he gave me his ass to kiss. I didn't do anything wrong. Our love was strong, but Quinnzel wasn't ready to stop being a thug and be a man point blank. His wimp- ass couldn't even look at me when he said good-bye. Damn. I'm not ready to let Quinnzel go, but I guess I don't have a choice. He had DeShawn pick up his things and drop off my keys, and every night since is filled with loneliness. And the silence is so loud. I definitely feel the void inside. I've been listening to *One Last Cry* on repeat. Ironically, there seems to be no end to my tear fetish. Dezionne is on her way to temporally rescue me from my pity party. She has been staying with her mom since the fire and talking about moving to Maryland with DeShawn. I don't know who's going to die for the blaze, but knowing Supreme it will be somebody. Yeah, I'm bitter right now. What!?!

Me and Dezionne hit up Jillian's, our usual spot. Everything was flowing until she mentioned the Q word.

"Dezionne, don't go there."

"Nae, y'all are pitiful apart."

"No, we're worlds apart."

"Just call him."

"Sure I won't. Quinnzel dissed me. I only play the fool one time."

"So you're going to isolate yourself from civilization."

"Nope, from Quinnzel's heart-ache."

"Imani?"

"Dezionne, he hurt me."

"I thought pain was love."

I sat back in my seat and found the truth in Dezionne's cynical remark.

"Imani, Quinnzel never stopped loving you. He's trapped and you are his light."

I couldn't stop my tears from falling. Dezionne held my hand from across the table.

"I have to let him go."

"Nae, Quinnzel will die without you. I'm telling you this because he is my brother and I love him. You gave him a reason to live."

"Why is all this about Quinnzel," I said wiping my nose. "He shitted on me."

"Imani, do you love Quinnzel?"

"Obviously. I'm crying a river over this fool."

"Then don't lose him over his bullshit ass pride, or yours. Go get your man girl."

"I'm not ready."

Dezionne got up and sat next to me.

"Nae, I know you're hurting. But don't wallow in your misery for too long."

"Misery loves company."

"You know I got your back all day. But I'm not miserable, I got dick in my life."

We laughed and Dezionne hugged me.

"Imani, you need Quinn as much as he needs you."

"What am I going to do?"

"Listen to your heart and your rusty pussy."

We cracked up. Dezionne ordered another round and went to the bathroom. Damn. I don't want to think about Quinnzel anymore. He took my love for granted and I'm not sure I want to be the bigger person. If I do holla at Quinnzel, it won't be any time soon. I appreciate Dezionne's concern but her pep talk is directed to the wrong person. We chilled for a while and were ready to go. Two cuties stepped to us on the way out.

"Ms. Lady, can I approach. I'm Joey."

"Imani."

"Imani you are gorgeous. Can I have your autograph?"

Dezionne sucked her teeth. She gave his bull no play. Joey paid her no mind and macked on.

"Imani, I would like to see you again."

I pulled out a business card with my home number on the back.

"Call me."

We walked out to the parking lot to Dezionne's car. She didn't say much on the ride to my place.

"Imani," Dezionne said before I got out. "Don't get caught up."

"What are you talking about?"

"Think about it. I'll see you tomorrow."

I closed the door and she pulled off. I went inside and took a bath. I put on my pj's and got in my empty bed. The phone rang and I jumped at the thought of it being Quinnzel.

"Hello."

"Hello, may I speak to Imani?"

"It's me, who's speaking."

"Joey."

"Hi."

"What's up mama, how you?"

"I'm good."

"Imani look, the mood was kind of tense tonight with your girl tripping."

"She's protective."

"I'm not trying to hurt you shorty, I just want to chill."

"Chill?"

"Yeah, where you be I be. You know."

His boyish style amused me.

"Joey, how old are you?"

"Old enough to do whatever you want."

"Yeah. What do you do?"

"Construction."

We talked for a while before I said good night. I told Joey he could take me to dinner tomorrow. Shit, I thought Quinnzel was my cause and cure but I can't stress over him anymore. Damn that. I went to sleep with hopes of a new beginning.

I spent Tuesday securing sponsors for the talent showcase. I confirmed Reebok, Dunhpy Nisaan, First Union, and of course And One. Plus the Hot Boyz will be broadcasting live from the Liacouras Center. I still need a hot entertainer to rock the stage. Everybody is doing they thing right now. The ROC, Murder Inc, Nelly, Eve, and the kids love Bow-Wow, and B2K. Maybe I can ask DeShawn to look out. I know he does the concerts way big at the Palace. He has to have some connects. I got booths for AIDS and breast cancer awareness to be set up in the lobby and the give-a-ways are going to be crazy. Club Synergy is hype for the show, practicing twice as long. Dezionne left at three today for rehearsal. Her dedication is honorable. As a matter of fact, I'm presenting her with a plaque of honorable mention for outstanding community service after the show.

I left the office at six and went up to Willow Grove Mall. I browsed in Vicki and copped a Coach bag from Macys'. I got to my dads' house at seven-thirty. I told Joey to pick me up here. He gave me too many frivolous responses for his words to be true. So, if dude pops up with some unwarranted issues he'll have to holla at daddy's sawed off shoty with the scope. I opened the door and smelled homemade rolls baking.

"Daddy." I walked back to the kitchen.

Mrs. Ilene came from behind the counter and hugged me.

"How are you baby doll?"

"I'm fine Mrs. Ilene," I said brushing the flour from her apron off of my coat. "Is my dad here?"

"No, he had some errand to run."

"Okay. I'll be upstairs."

"Are you expecting someone?"

"Yes."

"That handsome fellow you was flaunting at the hospital."

She had to go there,

"No, Mrs. Ilene. Quinnzel and I broke up."

I didn't give her a chance to respond. I left the kitchen and went upstairs. I smiled to myself. My dad kept my room the same way I had it back in the day. Pictures, posters, and teddy bears everywhere. Every time I'm in here, I'm reminiscing. I laid my white suede Prada pant suit on my bed. I took a quick shower and got dressed. Mrs. Ilene came in while I was curling my hair.

"Imani, I'm not trying to trouble you chile but I have something to say."

I turned around on my stool and Mrs. Ilene sat on my bed.

"Sugar that man made you glow."

"Now I'm crying his tears."

"Imani you're missing my point. Quinnzel reached your soul, no one else will. Sure you'll find another man and he may love you, but Quinnzel was genuine. He gave you bliss. That's an impossible act to follow. There is no substitute for true love."

"How do you know all that?"

"Ask yourself that question."

I slumped my shoulders and closed my eyes. Mrs. Ilene rubbed my face.

"Imani you are beautiful," she said. "You have the strength of Kings in your wings. Don't be afraid to go after what you want. You belong with that man."

"Thank you Mrs. Ilene."

"Honey hush." She kissed my cheek. "Don't let go of your love Imani. He knows your worth. Believe me."

Mrs. Ilene hugged me and went back downstairs. I sat there in tranquility. I want Quinnzel to come save me but that's a dream deferred. I haven't heard from him since he closed the door on us. It's funny; I never worried about time with Quinnzel because I thought we had forever. But shit got flipped. Forever evidently wasn't our forecast judging by the bruise on my heart. But that can't be right; our good out weighs the bad. The doorbell rang fucking up my rotation. Damn.

I spent a dry evening with Joey at Holahan's. My Quinnzel hex stole the night from him. Plus baby face couldn't even order my drink. He can't handle me. And what kind off nineteen-year-old construction worker drives a classic Mercedes Benz. Niggas will beat you in the head with anything they can as long as it sounds good. The truth is too much like right. Joey fucked up completely when we rolled out and he offered to take me to a movie. Mommy told me any man who takes you to a movie on your first date wants the darkness to last for the rest of the night. True.

"I'm cool. You can take me back to my spot."

"What's up sexy, you don't want to cruise?"

Time to shut him down.

"Sweetie, I cruise all day. I'm just not feeling you."

"Oh it's like that. Get the fuck out."

We just got off of Lincoln Drive. Joey pulled over next to Picket.

"Please don't drop me off here. I'll get out, but not here."

"Bitch do I look like I give a fuck. Get out."

I opened the door and got out. Joey peeled down Wayne Avenue. I saw Derek on top of me in the dark shadows. I remembered my horrified spirit. I heard Quinnzel telling me 'be strong Imani. I never thought I would need him desperately, damn it I do now. This man told me he would die for me. Come on weeping willow Imani, here comes the 65 bus.

Quinnzell Supreme Sharpe

I told Malik about Imani. Soon as that nigga came back hype as shit about their meeting, I knew he would try and get at her. I cut that shit short early. Shit, nobody on my team can fuck anything I claimed. That's the rules. The smut jawns, niggas can hit them all day. Not Imani, we shared too much. Last month commemorated one year with Imani. Damn I fucked up. I know I did. But Imani is still my my future wife; nothing is going to change that. I'm just not coming back at her until I've established myself the way I need to be to marry her.

"What's the business Quinn," Dezionne said sitting across from me in my booth.

I'm relaxing with the VIP crowd.

"Shit. What's the deal?"

Dezionne twisted her face all crazy when half butt-naked Shakera eased in the booth next to me.

"Step Pocahontas," Dezionne said making Shakera feel the reality of her bite.

She bounced quicker than AI flying down court.

"I'm cooling Quinn. Where's my man?"

Dezionne's proper as shit. She didn't dwell on the non-sense.

"Office." I poured Dez a drink.

"Thanks. You call Imani yet?"

"Dez, damn."

"My bad. Smut after skank-ass smut is much better than a loving companion. Fuck is wrong with me?"

"Dez, you know what it is."

"Quinn, you give up the street dream for a woman like Imani. I thought you knew that."

I ain't say shit.

"It's cool. Just let her keep chilling with Joey."

"Who the fuck is Joey?"

"Joey from the Eastside," Malik said walking up to the table. "Imani's sleeping with the enemy dog. Holla at me."

Imani's fucking with Joey. This shit ain't supposed to go down like this.

"Yo 'Preme, shit is constitutional, controversial, and complicated."

"Let's walk. Dez I'll be right back," I said raising up. "Stay here."

Me and Malik got on the elevator and went outside. We walked around back to the office. I unlocked the gate and Malik followed me inside. De blasted the eight ball off of the table and looked up.

"What's the deal my niggas?"

"Feds may have us on candid camera," Malik said.

De smiled.

"I heard, shit is hot. Have a seat."

We sat at the roundtable on some Godfather shit. It's not sweet.

"Break it down 'Lik," De said lighting a cigarette.

I know he already got some shit from Rahiem.

"Two rotating vans from eleven to seven."

"Don't forget Blalock creeping," De said.

"That pussy sleeping with the fishes yesterday."

De looked at Malik and laughed.

"The game remains the same," I said slamming my hand on the table. "Joey's nut-ass is with my lady."

"What the fuck," De said looking at me all crazy. "You was been supposed to dead that dumb shit Q."

"Your life ain't my life."

"That's where you're wrong baby boss," De said gritting on me. "You think you're doing this shit by yourself. Nigga you ain't shit. One, all you have is us. Two, all you need is your lady muthfucka. If you ain't going to play don't fuck with it."

I looked at De with no words to speak. Malik broke the tense silence.

"I hate to break up this touching family moment," he said. "But I got shit on stand-by."

"I'm a hit up the sixty-second assassin," De said sitting back in his seat.

"Not yet. Let me check some shit out first," Malik said. He stood up.

"What you got."

"You know me Money. I keep my enemies close nigga watch my homies."

"I heard that."

"I'm out."

"Yo use the escape route dog," De said. "Matter of fact hold up I see my bosom in VIP."

De and Malik went upstairs and I sat there floating up shits creek. I let my lady fall prey to a rival muthfucka. My mind gots to be playing tricks on me. A minute ago shit was lovely. How the fuck did I get here, the muthfucking G funk. I got up and picked up the phone. I called Imani and she wasn't there. Fuck a message, a drive-by is necessary. I went upstairs to tell to De I'm out. He and Dez were all hugged up in the booth.

"Yo, I'll be back."

"Tell Imani I said holla," De said. He got up and gave me a pound.

Dezionne smiled at me.

"I schooled you well young grasshopper."

"What's art without a paintbrush?"

I hugged Dezionne and she kissed my cheek.

"Bring my girl home," Dezionne said.

I turned to walk away.

"Quinn."

"What's up?"

"Don't stop until she's speaking in tongues."

"Please believe me."

I rolled to Imani's crib. It was after midnight Her Bentley is in her parking space so I know she's in the crib. I don't want to ring the buzzer so I waited for a tenant to go inside. Shit, I wanted to wait 'cause patience is a virtue. But what I have established with Imani I can let no nigga put us under. Fuck that. I knocked on Imani's door hoping she wouldn't dismiss me. Imani opened the door wearing the robe I gave her in Maryland. Damn, she is still gorgeous.

"Come in Quinnzel."

Imani is provocative. That's a quality few women garter. I followed Imani inside and we sat on the couch. She looked at me and I saw forever in her eyes.

"Imani, I made a mistake," I said. "I had a lot on my mind. I apologize. I want us to be together for as long as we can be."

She didn't say anything.

"Imani, I just want to love you. Is that okay?"

Imani bit her bottom lip and closed her eyes. I took her hands from her lap and held them in mine. Imani opened her eyes and smiled real sexy-like.

"Let's make this happen."

I kissed Imani and savored each passing minute. I say goddamn. She made my spirit light. No more faded pictures, nothing else matters. I know now I have to maintain balance between life on the block and my women. Yamean, it's essential. Every thug needs a lady. I'm not letting mines go ever. I didn't ask any questions about Joey. I learned a long time ago never to ask a question I don't want to know the answer to. Besides, anything Imani did while I was acting like a dickhead, I brought that. So what's the next best thing, dick her muthfucking head off. I devoured Imani with hot, sweaty, passionate sex. I killed that shit with my stroke game. I even hit her with a 69 yeah.

"Imani."

"What's up baby?"

"I almost fucked up our ordinance."

"Almost doesn't count." Imani laid her head on my chest. "Did you say ordinance?"

I laughed.

"Yeah this is something Heaven ordained."

"I love you too." I kissed Imani's forehead. "Quinnzel?"

"Yes."

"Why did you walk away from us?"

There was no escaping that question.

"I thought I was losing myself."

"I made you feel that way?"

I sat up and she sat up with me.

"Imani, I was tripping off myself. You complete me; there will never be another for me."

"You better realize."

"I love you too."

"Q, all I want from you is what you are."

"I'm all for it because all I am, is a man in love with you. This is the only place I want to be."

I held Imani and we went to sleep. The storm is over. I got up early and made Imani breakfast. Before she left for work I stopped her at the door. I whispered I'm in love with you, girl. She rushed over to me.

"Will you be here when I get home," She said shaking.

"I promise."

She kissed me and rolled out. I heard my two-way ringing in the bedroom. I checked the message, it said: OFFICE. I threw on my gear and looked like yesterday. It's cool, I'm chill with yesterday. Yesterday, I restored order. I rolled to the Palace to holla at my niggas. De knew what it was when he saw me.

"Nigga handled his shit." I gave De a pound.

"You know it." I sat on the couch next to Malik. "What's up nigga?"

"You," he said giving me a pound. "Yo, 'Preme on the real keep it tight with your shorty seriously."

"No question. What's popping though?"

De sat in the side chair and lit his cigarette.
"Stan is snitching." Shit.
"Snitches get stitches."
"Fuck around and end up in ditches."
"Set that shit off."

Imani

Gangster love is vicious. A broken love can break your spirits. Bottom-line; if you want your man, don't act like you don't. Quinnzel is the owner of my heart, how could we ever be apart. We're back in effect, now I can breathe again.

I wore a leopard Gucci suit Friday night to host our first annual talent showcase. The capacity crowd in the Liacouras Center rocked every minute with Club Synergy. The dance ensemble just blazed the stage with a hot set. I walked back to the podium pumping my fists.

"Yeah give it up."

Thunderous applause roared from the standing crowd.

"That's what's up," I said cueing the light change. "We're going to keep the show moving. Let's make this noise for the world's most talented record label, Murder INC."

The deafening ovation echoed and spread like a mantra. Murder INC tore it down, no question. Nas came out spitting. Charli B-More held it down. You know Chuck rep Philly. Miss Ashanti did her thing as usual. And Ja, no words are needed except R-U-L-E. Please no hateration. I give props where props are due. If you do your thing, I'll hold you down. I came on stage and greeted the entourage after their finale.

"Holla," I said hugging my guests.

No one in the place was seated. Ja presented me with a leather autographed Murder Inc jacket.

"It's murder," I said holding the jacket up. "That's what I'm talking about. Give it up for Murder INC, they did the damn thing."

I thanked Ja and the INC left the stage to deserving acclamation.

"Whoa, that was crazy. I want to thank everyone who made this happen tonight. Our success derives from your support. It takes a village to raise a child."

I paused for the applause.

"I would like to take this opportunity to acknowledge the woman who dedicates her time to teaching and uplifting our children. She inspires our youth to achieve and to form aspirations. She gives them courage to strive for their dreams in an otherwise society of prejudice. Please join me in recognizing an overly impressive woman, Dezionne Sinclair."

Dezionne came from back stage baffled. I gave her the plaque and she broke down. I hugged my girl and the crowd gave love too. DJ Flow fired up the beats and Club Synergy came on stage jamming. Right on cue, balloons and confetti sprinkled across the stage from the risers. The final fireworks blew and Club Synergy shouted, 'Thank you Philly'. We applauded the crowd as they headed for the exits. Reporters for channels 3,6,10, Fox, and the Daily News straggled behind for interviews. I addressed the press while the clean up crew did their thing. Once I finished my comments, I joined the post performance celebration back stage.

Friends and family partied with the Club and grubbed on pizza and Buffalo wings. Me and Dezionne chilled at our table with the fam. Including Jovan, unfortunately. Daddy and Mrs. Ilene called it a night.

"Congratulations Nae Nae and to you to Dezionne," Dad said.

He put on his coat and hat.

"I'll call you tomorrow Daddy," I said hugging him. "Much love."

My dad shook Quinnzel's hand and gave Amir a hug before he and Mrs. Ilene left. Some dude in a black dickie suit bumped his way to our table.

"Jovan." Oh shit was her expression but words were not her

friend. "What you don't hear me?"

"Who is this clown," Amir said grilling Jovan.

"Clown, nigga I'll fuck you up."

"Please," I said standing up. "There are children in here."

I looked at Jovan. She was slumped down in her seat with her eyes closed, like if she can't see us we can't see her.

"Jovan you need to handle this," I said blowing her cover.

She sucked her teeth.

"Amir this is Greg, Hakiem's father," Jovan said whining like a baby.

"I ain't ask for no muthfucking introduction," Greg said. "Bring your ass girl."

Hakiem is Jovan's youngest son. The older two have the same father who I'm going to assume is also homicidal. Jovan sat there like she was stuck. I looked at my brother. His bloodshot eyes and flinching jaw told me he's about to wile out. Amir sized Greg up.

"Yo brother," Quinnzel said. "We don't want any problems."

Yeah baby.

"Did I ask you?"

Oh shit, this could get ugly. I know my man.

"Baby don't," I said.

DeShawn put his hand under the table. Dezionne stood up and told the parents it's time to go. She obviously knows her man too. Dezionne commended the club and told them to enjoy the week off. Parents came over to shake my hand not knowing I'm in the middle of a shit storm. I went to the door and stood next to Dezionne to accept gratitude on the walk-by. I kept my Coach bag on my shoulder. Since the rape, I carry a big clip that'll get niggas off me. Fuck the dumb shit. Me and Dez stayed at the door even after everyone cleared out.

"Are you going to roll too pussy," Greg said to Amir.

"Niggas from the ville never ran, never will."

Amir jumped up and he and Greg started boxing. Amir was dogging him. Dude ate punches in the grill and took mad body shots. Q and DeShawn stood up, hyping Amir up like they were watching a heavy weight bout.

"Stop that shit," Dezionne said.

She heard my thoughts. Jovan sat in the chair shaking.

"Don't hurt my baby's dad."

"Your baby's dad, bitch is you crazy…"

Dezionne grabbed me; my girl knew what time it was. Amir and Greg tussled on the ground and Q and DeShawn looked for an opening. Greg reached down to his ankle and pulled a gun out of his boot. Before he could work the safety he had three guns at his dome.

"You blaze, we blaze," I said with my finger on the nickel-plated trigger.

Jovan screamed and jumped up out of her chair. She ran to Greg and covered him with her body. Amir stood up and I walked over to him with my heat still seeking.

"Get your mark ass up out of here before you get dealt with," Amir said.

Jovan and Greg picked themselves up from the floor.

"Amir," Jovan said.

"Shut the fuck up," Amir said with no hesitation. "Roll, because you're done."

Jovan grabbed her bag off of the table and ran to the door. Dezionne tripped her ass on the way out. She smacked the floor and her skin slid on the tile. Greg walked backwards to the door.

"Supreme."

Quinnzel looked surprised. He twisted his face.

"Nigga you don't know me."

"You don't know what the fuck I know. I'll let Joey know your bitch-ass is still in commission. We thought 5-0 had you shook!"

"That's what you get for thinking. My heart doesn't pump kool-aide. Ain't shit sweet about me."

"We'll see."

"Nigga pick your bitch up off the floor and bounce,"

DeShawn said stepping in front of Quinnzel.

DeShawn walked to the door and followed Greg out. I'm tripping off of this shit. A security guard came in and told me the clean up was complete. We got our shit together and rolled to the Palace.

Quinnzell Supreme Sharpe

Imani is straight ride or die. When she pulled out that sweet ass forty-five on Greg, I wanted to freak her right there, yamean. I don't even care that she got me out here like a sucker shopping for pads. Always ultra-thin overnights with wings, the orange tab. Imani got that shit down to a science. I picked up her pads and went to the register. The counter girl cracked on me. She looks like a fucking crayon with her pink hair and purple eyes.

"I'm saying cutie, what do I have to do to get with you?"

"One yourself sis."

I took my change and walked outside to my ride. Before I could get in niggas stepped to me.

"Thomas and Williams, what the fuck y'all niggas want?"

"This is the part where you come with us young blood," Thomas said.

"You said that shit like we peoples."

"Shithead," Williams said. "Either you get in on your own or you know the rest."

"Damn Butch Diesel, is it like that," I said laughing. "You got it, I don't want no work. We can ride."

I got in their fly-ass Infiniti on some calm cool and collected type shit. I don't know what's going down but I'm a play it real smooth. They took me down to the roundhouse and left me in an interrogation room. Jovan walked in wearing a three-piece suit.

"Oh shit, you're a cop? I knew it was a reason I didn't like your slimy ass"

She sat down in front of me.

"DEA to be a bit more precise." Jovan opened her file folder. "I'm going to ask you some real simple questions."

"Simple like do you see my lawyer?"

"What makes you think you need one? You're not under arrest."

"You're questioning me right."

"Quinnzel," she said flipping pages. "Steven Peterson's body was recovered last night. I believe his street name was Blalock. Peterson was rival to Joseph Stanton. I believe you know him."

"So?"

"I need you to infiltrate Stanton's operation."

"Joey's operation?" So they don't know, I'm in the crack game.

"Yes."

"No."

"Okay. What can you tell me about Shawn Porter's disappearance?"

Jovan dropped a black and white of me and Nino on the table in front of me. Damn.

"You decide which case you want to discuss."

"I ain't discussing shit."

"Really? Maybe you're interested in hearing what Tasha Stewart had to say."

I don't believe this shit.

"You're trying to stick me to some missing person's bullshit unless I help you with a drug bust."

"Murder one to be exact."

"How you figure that?"

"Tasha isn't my only witness."

Shit Stan.

"I'll give you forty-eight hours to decide."

"It ain't shit to decide. You're the cop, do your own fucking job."

Never let them see you sweat.

"So unless you got my lawyer in your back pocket, I'm out."

I stood up and went to the door.

"Do you love Imani?"

I turned around and looked at Jovan. She smiled at me.

"I know you do. It's too bad it'll be 25 to life before she'll see you again."

"Do what you feel."

I opened the door and walked down the hallway. Nobody followed me. They ain't got no evidence. Yet. They're coming for my head but it ain't going down like that. I paged De and Malik and told them to bring their asses. I jumped in a cab and went to O'Hara's. I was on my fourth drink when Malik came in.

"What the deal my nigga," he said sitting down.

"It's grimy on the block. Jovan is a muthfucking."

"Amir's shorty? That's fucked up."

"I know this."

"Yo feel this, if she blew her cover they're running out of time." Malik lit a cigarette. "Why they come at you though?"

"She said to knock Joey off."

"Hold up Q something don't add up."

"What you mean?"

Before he could say shit De walked up spilling.

"Yo niggas, I just left Rahiem and shit is grimy."

"That must be the theme for the day," I said giving De a pound.

He sat down and lit a cigarette.

"That bull Greg," De said. "Was a decoy for the Feds. He was supposed to see how much we knew about Joey."

"And Jovan is DEA," I said.

"Stop fucking playing."

"I laugh and joke but I don't play."

"Alright," Malik said. "If they need Q they ain't got shit on us."

"They got Stan."

"Oh shit," squad said in chorus.

"Chill my niggas. They want me to help bring Joey down, that's all."

"So they don't know y'all got beef," De said.

"Nah, they think he smoked Blalock."

"So why they come at you?"

"That's the same shit I said," Malik said giving De a pound.

I sat back and remembered Jovan's words.

"Yo she's going to use Imani to get me."

"How you figure that?" Malik looked confused.

"I was at Imani's crib when I talked to Tasha a minute ago. She came at me real greasy. I know her fucking phone was tapped."

"That don't mean shit baby boss."

"Instincts lead me to this flow dog."

"So what the fuck?"

"Yo," Malik said standing up. "Let me holla at my peoples. With shit deep like this they definitely know some shit."

"We got to meet at the park later, change the profile up," I said giving Malik a pound.

"Hit me up. Keep your mind right. I'm ghost."

Malik gave De a pound and rolled.

"That nigga came back on the set right on time," I said.

"No muthfucking doubt."

"Yo, take me to get my whip so I can holla at wifey."

"Let's be out."

De drove up to the PathMark on Wayne & Chelten.

"Fuck you were doing shopping," De said. "What you're Benson now?"

"Fuck you nigga, I only got some pads."

De cracked up.

"Mini or maxi, what you take?"

"That shit is funny?"

"Yo Imani got you copping pads. You need to put a name to her straight up."

"It'll be what it is. I'm out."

"Alright. I'll hit you up to see what's crackulating."

I gave De a pound and rolled to Imani's crib. She was sitting out on the balcony.

"You left here five hours ago Quinnzel."

Imani didn't even look at me when she spoke. I kneeled in front of her.

"Imani, how much do you love me?" She smiled.

"It's not the quantity it's the quality."

"Imani I'm serious."

"What's going on?"

"Jovan is DEA."

"That's fucked up. She must have crazy tabs on you. Shit."

Imani got up and I followed her inside. I grabbed her and put my arms around her. I might as well put all the shit out there. What don't come out in the wash comes out in the rinse.

"Imani listen. A lot of treacherous shit goes down in the street. But I need you to know I never killed anybody."

"Is that what this is about?"

"Pieces."

"It's Nino isn't it?"

"Imani, leave the block alone. I just need you to trust me."

"I do and I believe you."

"That's what I'm talking about. Nobody has my back like you do."

"You better know it. I will always hold you down."

"I knew you were a gangster on the EL."

"The only thug in the hood that was strong enough to claim you."

Imani took me to the bedroom and put that shit on me. We laid back and Imani pulled out the chessboard.

"You know you done fucked up? I don't know why you do it to yourself."

"Q what makes you think you can beat me?"

"Just set it up."

Imani set the board up and I ordered some grub. Before she could make her first move my two-way went off.

"It's De, I got to go."

"Damn babe."

"My bad Beloved."

"Nigga get to stepping and cut the corner."

"It's like that?"

Imani laughed.

"Never like that."

I got up and threw my gear on.

"I'll be back."

Imani kissed me and held me close.

"I love you. Be safe, it's real out there."

"I got you." Imani walked me to the door. "I'll see you tonight."

"I'll be waiting face down ass up."

"That's my girl."

I closed the door and bounced. I rolled to Aubury Park. De and Malik were waiting for me on the basketball court. We walked through the park to the woods.

"Dig the move niggas," Malik said. "Joey is on some Pablo Escobar shit in the drug game. Feds need him like yesterday but they can never get shit to stick."

"Tell Blaze to take this nigga off the map," I said.

"If it was that easy the Feds wouldn't need you Q."

"So what you saying," De said.

"I'm saying we're going to have to set that nigga up for failure," Malik said. "Snatch up his peoples, make him come to us."

"To help 5-0, nigga please."

"To help us. This nigga is 'bout to aim hired guns in our direction."

"What are you talking about," De said.

"My man Banks is Joey's marksman. If we toss that nigga some bigger dollars he's good. But there may be some other niggas who aren't so easily persuaded."

"Alright look. I'm a holla at Rahiem to see what's popping," De said. "But uh, they ain't stop making guns when they made theirs so if these niggas want it they can come get it."

"I'm a go to the block to keep shit settle," Malik said.

"Yo Lik."

"What's up Money?"

"Good looking out. You keep niggas on point for real."

"For real," I said.

"No doubt," Malik said. "We're all in the same game. I'm a get at y'all niggas."

We walked back to our wheels.

"I got to go scoop Dez up from her moms crib," De said.

"Cool. I'll be at Imani's."

"Bet. We'll come through."

De gave me a pound and rolled out. I got in the whip and went to the Palace to check shit. I picked up the loot for Dezionne to deposit and rolled back out. I balled down the expressway. I peeped some niggas tailing me. I hit the drive and those niggas are still on me. I pulled over in Sunoco and got out. Fuck that chasing me shit. A black Infiniti pulled up beside me. Thomas and Williams got out and leaned against my whip.

"What the fuck man, why are y'all sweating me?"

"You know what young blood," Thomas said. "I would hate to have another nigga fucking my woman."

"Especially a woman like yours Sharpe," Williams said. "She's thicker than a snicker."

"What the fuck is your point?"

"McMillan," Williams said.

"Who?"

"Derek McMillan," Thomas said. "We give you Derek, you give us Joey."

"What is this, a set up?"

"It's a bargain shithead."

"Well let me think about it ass cheek."

Williams threw me against the car and pinned his arm under neck.

"You think you tough. Well I got something for you. We're going to get Joey and then we're coming for you. I know the deally yo."

"Get the fuck off me."

"So what's it going to be Sharpe," Thomas said.

"I said I'll think about it."

"Solid. But remember this young blood, a blind man can't see."

"No shit Sherlock."

Imani

For my man; I would lie for him. Anything - if he need bail, I'd front the cash for him, hide the stash for him, getaway drive for him, ride for him, hold it down for him, buss shots in enemies, seize memories of quiet nights by his side, fight to the death. I'm Bonnie to his Clyde. I'm down to swing as long as Quinnzel is my love. I'll do whatever I have to do to keep him. Quinnzel set my soul on fire. And I'm not interested in loving anybody else. The only thing that matters is the way Quinnzel makes me feel inside, outside, up side, down side. Damn. With the slightest touch, with one look in my eyes I fall in love with Quinnzel all over again. Love is like wet dreams come true all day. I worship Quinnzel with his ruff-neck ass. Eat, sleep, shit, fuck, eat, sleep, shit, then its back to the street to make a buck quick. MC Lyte called it from back in the day. And when all is said and done, every thug needs a lady.

I went in the office early Thursday morning. I got ballers coming in who want to hook up with me as their agent. I was like stop playing when the proposition first came at me. Now I'm like hell yeah. This is something major to add to the repertoire. I keep all opportunities flowing freely. Since the regular season is over and the draft isn't until the end of June, I can concentrate on sealing endorsements for my clients before we embark on summer camps and clinics. Boom. Let the negotiations begin.

"Okay peach Imani," Dezionne said when I walked in. "Work it out."

"I do what I do like I'm doing it for NC17."

"Holla."

Dezionne followed me in my office and sat on the couch.

"What are you doing here so early Dez?"

"Confirming guest speakers, food, and music for the benefit Saturday night."

We organized a charity for battered women and children. We're going to host monthly bazaars with raffles to fund raise for low-income homes, medical and dental coverage, and childcare.

"That's what's up. We're at the Clef Club right?"

"You know it. Oh, you're starting to get calls from owners of NFL teams."

"Alright boom, the ill cross over. The NFL is territory I've been waiting to reign over. Training camps should be starting soon, so I got to make those moves ASAP. What's next?"

"Sixers party."

"We have to push that back to July. Maybe make it something big with the 4th or AI's celebrity classic softball game."

"I could feel that if we hook it up right."

"Now what's my name?"

"N to the A to the E in the hisouse."

"Whose house," I said doing the whop. "Boom. We need a venue."

"I'm on it."

Dezionne got up and went to her desk. I picked up the bios to review the backgrounds of my potential clients who ball in the NBA already. And because I'm so clever, I have clout at the draft so I can get exclusive with 1st and 2nd round draft picks who aspire to be future hall of famers.

Dezionne buzzed my phone.

"What up?"

"Some morning nutrients."

"I got a ten o' clock."

"Nae its seven thirty."

"Boom. Let's roll."

I went out front and me and Dezionne walked down the hall to the elevator. The doors opened and Jovan stood there like shit on a stick. She flashed her badge.

"Ladies, let's reminisce."

"About you fucking my brother or me beating your ass?"

"How about you in an orange jumpsuit." Jovan stepped out of the elevator. "This is Tasha Stewart. I believe you two are already acquainted. Let's walk."

I looked at Dezionne. She winked at me. Alright fuck it. Let's play. We walked back to my office to the conference room.

"So Imani," Jovan said.

"Call me Ms. Best." She smiled.

"Fine. Ms. Best how long do you think it will take before Quinnzel considers you to be expendable?"

"What?"

"This may come as a surprise but it seems as if people who were once close to him somehow come up missing."

Jovan put pictures of Nino and Cash on the table in front of me. But Nino killed Cash.

"You think Quinnzel…" Jovan cut me off.

"Quinnzel is a malicious murderer," she said. Jovan looked at Dezionne. "And an acclaimed drug dealer like his big brother."

"Prove it," Dezionne said giving Jovan an ill ice grill.

"Oh I will," Jovan said. Dezionne challenged Jovan.

"Since you're Ms. Big Shit Detective who burned down my house?"

Jovan sat back in her chair. Got her, get her out.

"The explosive used to blow up your house was highly sophisticated. Actually its use is not authorized in this country."

"Meaning you don't have a fucking clue," Dezionne said.

"I'm confident that when I find the assassin I'll nail the bomber as well. Kill two birds with one stone." Jovan cut her eyes at me. "Unless of course you want to prove me wrong Imani, uh Ms. Best."

"Excuse me."

"You think Quinnzel is innocent help me court another suspect."

"Hell no," Dezionne said. "Investigate your own bullshit."

"Ms. Best I didn't know you had ventriloquist skills."

"Wench you didn't just call me a talking dummy."

Dezionne jumped up. I grabbed her before she fucked around and caught a case.

"Jovan, I think you should roll because you're done," I said.

She stood up and put her card on the table.

"Tell Amir I said hello." She and Tasha walked to the door. "Ms. Best consider my offer. I believe you have some unfinished business of your own with Mr. Stanton."

"Who?"

"You'll see. I'll be in touch."

Dezionne followed Jovan and Tasha out. I walked around the table to Jovan's chair. I picked up a black and white of me and Joey at Holahans from her seat. Oh shit. I put the photo in my briefcase and went out front.

"I'm scared Nae," Dezionne said. She stood motionless at the window.

"It'll be cool Dez."

"Come on Imani. She's talking about drug trafficking and murder. And in our backward ass bullshit society the constitution is null and void. You're guilty until proven innocent."

"What if I help Jovan?"

"What?" Dezionne turned around with tears in her eyes. "Imani she's trying to set you up. There is no other suspect."

I walked over to Dezionne and hugged her. She cried on my shoulder.

"I can't lose my family behind this bullshit Nae. I've lost too much already."

"It's okay Dez. We'll let Q and DeShawn know what's up and come up with some new moves to make."

The phone rang bringing us back to Miracle Media leaving our drama on pause for the moment.

We made it through the rest of the day with ease. At seven o' clock DeShawn and Q met us at Zanzibar Blue. I told Dezionne to let me do all the talking about Jovan. She's working with a lot of emotions so it's my time to hold it down.

"Babe, Jovan came to the office today."

"Huh," Quinnzel and DeShawn said together.

"If you can huh you can hear," Dezionne said.

"Dez," I said shaking my head.

"My bad, do you."

"What's the deal Imani," DeShawn said.

"Really she was just trying to gas me up."

"She assassinated my character didn't she," Quinnzel said.

"I already love who you are babe." I kissed Quinnzel. "She's trying to put some bodies to y'all."

"Who?"

"Nino and Cash."

"I can finesse that," DeShawn said. "What else?"

"That's it. And she did have Tasha with her."

"Good looking," DeShawn said. "Q after you go to the block…"

"The block is hot," Dezionne said.

"It's cool boo, they don't know about the drug game."

"You're a damn lie," Dezionne said. "Jovan sat there and said Q is an acclaimed pusher like his big brother."

"What," Quinnzel said. "How the fuck she wants me to infiltrate some shit then?"

"She wants y'all to blast each other," DeShawn said.

"Oh she thinks I'm new to this, I got something for that ass. Let's roll peoples."

Quinnzel kissed me and told me he would see me tonight. DeShawn threw two bills on the table and they left. Dezionne went to the bathroom and I sat putting shit together. Jovan wants me to exonerate Quinnzel. She doesn't want Q, she wants Joey. And she used Quinnzel to get to me thinking that if Joey does something to Quinnzel I wouldn't have a choice but to help bring him down. Damn. Just call me the little lady from Murder She Wrote. Fuck that, Joey won't have a chance to blaze my dude.

I'm about to show y'all how Imani gets down, tiger style. I got up to use the phone. Dezionne passed me on the floor.

"Are you going to the bathroom?"

"Yeah then we're out."

"Cool. I need Calgon to take me away."

I used the pay phone to call Jovan.

"Jovan Price DEA."

"It's me."

"I've been expecting your call."

"It's on."

"Where should we meet?"

Quinnzell Supreme Sharpe

Malik got some grizzly niggas up in Pitt to shank Stan. He made it look like some prison beef over some cigarettes or soap or some shit. It's whatever as long as 5-0 can't connect my name to shit else. I'm good. Some ballistics evidence that disappeared is about to be found on Jovan's desk. The slugs from Cash to a gun registered to one Shawn Porter. We used their method against them. The judicial system has a way of losing evidence that doesn't support the prosecutor's case. We flipped it then reversed it, yamean. I definitely wasn't feeling Imani being in the middle of this shit. Jovan did her dirt. She tried to shake Imani, with nothing doing, so now she can leave her the fuck alone. I need to get my woman up out this game. Hold up. It's me who needs to get out the game. Damn. It's all fucked up now.

"Imani, you awake?"

"No."

I tickled Imani until she hit me with a pillow. She sat up.

"What's up babe?"

"I feel like we should get away from here," I said.

"Where would we go?"

"Africa."

"Okay Sincere," she said laughing. "Belly is my shit too."

I laughed.

"Seriously. We should just be out. Start a family."

"Uh...I want a husband not a baby daddy."

"I know, but this ain't no place to raise a family anyway."

"Quinnzel, I have a career here."

"You don't have to work."

"I have always had a job. I was a conductor on the freedom

train."

"Imani its not playtime, I'm serious. You just said you want a husband which means your job will be being my wife and raising our children."

"I don't know what to say."

"Imani, you are all I will ever need ain't shit going to change that. But right now you need to straighten out your priorities."

"So what, it's all or nothing?"

I shook my head.

"You can be Superwoman if you want to, I support you. But you don't have to take it there. Like I said priorities. Think about it."

"I will." Imani kissed my neck. "So what it is on the block?"

"Whoa slow down," I said. "I know you had your little run in with Jovan at your office, but that's a done deal. The block ain't for you. Come on ma, you already know what it is."

Imani turned over and laid down. Damn, she's feeling some type of way.

"Imani."

"What?" Damn.

"What's the deal?"

"Ain't shit, I'm sleepy."

I laid down and put my arm around her.

"Quinnzel, it's hot."

I moved my arm and turned around. Shit, what did I do? Imani was gone in the morning before I woke up. She didn't even cook me breakfast. A nigga done fucked up. But I ain't do shit. I said what I feel. Hold, let me pump my brakes. Imani doesn't let words take her off of her square. Especially real rap. Something else got her bugging. It could be her gig. She has been knocking it out something fierce from the gate. She elevated her game to the next level too, making new moves as an agent. She put a charity together, the draft's coming up, and she's about to add the NFL to her team. It's non-stop for the Huntress on a paper chase. I dig how Imani makes her moves. All of her

shit is on point. She don't have to change her game up for the
Bull. Imani's going to be my wife and I'm a be her right hand.
Fuck it. What nigga don't want a get money ryda on his team.
Let me let my Queen know I know what time it is and I'm repre-
senting by her side. Yeah. That's what the fuck is up.

I took a shower and threw on the Versace linen. I jumped in
the wheel to ride to Imani's office but something told me to shoot
through the block. Fuck it. I'm spontaneous I work on instinct. I
hopped on the drive and hit the E-way. I rode down Woodland
Avenue to the strip. 5-0 is out sickening. I peeped the crime
scene yellow tape on the block and saw niggas hemmed up all
crazy. Shit, that's Dennis, Mann, and Pookie. I looked down the
block and saw Kevin laid out. Damn not my man. Come on 5-0
not my fucking squad. Kev must've gone out blasting when those
niggas ran up in the spot. I got to see how they got the fuck up in
there. I hope them other niggas emptied the stash before 5-0
broke in. Fuck. This shit is way out of pocket. I can't even holla
at my eyes on the block to get the run down with 5-0 creeping. I
backed up and rolled out. Those niggas'll be hitting us up for the
bail paper in a minute. It ain't a thing as long as their story is
bulletproof. I laugh and joke but I don't play. Shit, fucking Pinky
and the Brain are on my ass again. I pulled into KFC on 52nd
Street and got out.

"What y'all niggas want man?"

"You don't run this shit bitch," Williams said. "You speak
when I tap your jaw."

"Tap these nuts in your mouth."

"Sharpe," Thomas said. "I believe we found what you have
been looking for."

"Fuck you talking about?"

"Let's go for a ride."

I got back in my wheel and followed those niggas. We wound
up at the Double Tree Hotel. I tucked the triplets low in position
and went to the penthouse.

"You want a drink," Thomas said.

"No. Let's handle business," I said with my back to the door. "What up?"

"No problem," Thomas said.

He nodded his head to Williams. He opened a closet door and threw some dude in the middle of the floor. He was tied up in cables.

"Derek McMillan meet Quinnzel Sharpe," Williams said. "Oh my bad its Preemie right."

"I'll be that. What the fuck is up with dude?"

Mind over matter Q. It's a reason they're anxious to put his blood on my hands.

"Come on Sharpe at least act like you know."

"Since when y'all been so willing to help me, what the fuck you get out this shit?"

"You get to keep breathing," Williams said. He pulled the chair from under the desk. "Sit down."

"I'm cool."

"No, you are not cool. Sit the fuck down."

I maintained my stance.

"Fine, we'll do it your way," Williams said. He pulled out his gun and emptied his clip in Derek's chest. "Skip the dramatics."

"Oh shit you're bugged the fuck out man," I said.

"Do I have your attention," Joey said coming from the bathroom clapping his hands.

"And what the fuck do you want?"

"I got a shipment coming in ten days and you are going to keep the cops off my ass."

"Ain't these two pricks your errand boys?"

"They are corrupt cops not decoys. And you answer questions don't ask."

"Somebody done told you wrong." I pulled out my Smith & Wesson's and aimed at Joey and Williams. "Back the fuck up."

Joey stepped back and raised his hands. He smiled.

"If I wanted you dead," Joey said. "You know the rest."

"Whatever nigga. I'm out."

"I'll see you in homicide division," Thomas said.

I held my targets.

"Fuck are you talking about?"

"Hello Derek McMillan," Thomas said laughing. "He raped your woman got out and bail and turns up dead. Open and shut case."

"What are you going to do, draw my fingerprints?"

"Mt. Laurel, New Jersey asshole," Williams said. "Info red light is a pretty eyed bitch. Like Imani."

"Imani," Joey said. "I know that bitch, ass like a bowl of Jell-O."

I bust two shots in the atmosphere.

"Y'all muthfuckas got something real to say or what?"

"Alright seize fire cat daddy," Joey said. "Meet me here tomorrow, eleven o' clock."

Joey tossed the hotel key card at my feet. I kept my gun on him and picked it up. I walked backwards to the door and opened it.

"Cat daddy you going to a fashion show," Joey said laughing. "Smack Imani's ass for me."

"My dick, bitch."

I jumped in the whip and rolled to Imani's crib. I paged De and Malik and told them to meet me there. De was sitting on the steps waiting for me. We went up. I opened a bottle of Corona and lost it. I threw the bottle against the refrigerator and knocked everything off of the counter. Glass broke everywhere.

"Q," DeShawn said grabbing me. "What the fuck is going on?"

"Joey's trying to get me." I pushed De off of me. "I got to handle that nigga."

"Quinn it's me dog. I'm on your side. What's up?"

"They killed Derek. They're trying to stick it to me. I meet him tomorrow eleven o' clock."

"Who the fuck is they?"

"Thomas and Williams."

"So what it is?"

"I'll find out what it's hitting for tomorrow."

"We're in there and now, that nigga need you."

"Let's set this shit up the right way. I'm trying to dead this fucker."

"It's gravy baby boss," De said. He put his arm around my neck. "We got this. But you better get this shit straight before wifey buss your ass early."

Imani

I met Jovan at Red Lobster's on Saturday night. Quinnzel felt some type of way when I told him I was going out. I can't let him know what's up. He's wanted to be up under me lately and I've been on some holla back shit. Only because I'm putting on big-ass fronts about where I'm going and what I'm doing. As much as I can't stand a lying ass man, I done flipped the script and dug my own dirt. But I'm trying to protect Quinnzel; I'm not lying for GP. That doesn't make it any easier. The friction is evident in our sex drive. Anytime something's not right in your relationship the lovemaking suffers the most.

"Imani," Jovan said. "I have good news and bad news."

"There is always a glitch in the program with you Jovan. Damn."

"You want to hear it or not?"

"Do I have a choice?"

"No."

"Then stop wasting my time asking bullshit questions you already know the answer to."

Jovan laughed.

"To be such a successful black business woman you are a real bitch."

"A superb female in control, thank you."

"Imani did you ever stop to think that your shit stinks too?"

"Yeah, but right now it's your shit that's halting progress so wipe your ass and clean yourself up."

"You're real cute. Anyway we have some leads but we also have some leaks."

"What else is new?"

"I want you to contact me using only this phone," Jovan said. She sat a cell phone on the table and slid it to me. "It's untraceable. Put it away."

"So what's the plan?"

"Work your shimmy. Get him to break down maybe he'll slip."

"Maybe? That's what I'm talking about glitch in the program."

"Imani we need to know what Joey's next move is, can you handle that?"

"Commence mission difficult."

"Good. The bag under the table has everything you'll need. Hidden cameras in watches, buttons, and belts, taps for you to leave in his place and car, and some other goodies."

"Goodies?" My eyes widened.

"Stun guns, smoke bombs, and hand grenades."

"Oh shit, fire power."

"I got your back."

"That's what your mouth says."

I started eating my shrimp.

"Imani, I'm sorry you have to go through this."

"We all do what we have to do don't we?"

"I never meant to hurt Amir."

"Of course not. You were so honest and sincere, how could he miss it. Please Jovan he was just a pawn in your business scheme."

"Imani…"

"Shut up."

"That sounds like a little more than bitterness. You want to talk about it?"

"With you? Hell no."

"Lying to someone you love is fucked up."

I didn't say anything.

"Imani I know. That's how I felt with Amir everyday and

everyday. I am sorry."

Jovan's pager went off.

"I have to go. Make sure you wear the cameras anytime you're going to meet up with Joey. And call me when the taps are in place."

"Not a minute sooner."

"Damn Imani. You know what you are going to need forgiveness one day and I hope whoever it is gives you their ass to kiss too."

"We can dream Jovan."

She shook her head.

"You be careful out there Ms. Best. It's not a game."

"Neither am I."

Jovan left and I sat there thinking about what she said. I mean for real for real you reap what you sow. Jovan knew she was lying to Amir. I know right now I'm the pot calling the kettle black, but I don't have a choice. Maybe Jovan felt she didn't have a choice either. Shit. See what happens when you let your conscience be your guide. You start feeling people you have never been eye to eye with. Damn sentimental bullshit.

I threw some money on the table, picked up my bags, and went home. I kept my secret mission bags in the trunk and went inside. Quinnzel's gone. Shit. I know he didn't drive all the way back to Maryland. I paged Quinnzel four times before he called me back.

"Where are you?"

"Damn Queen, what's up?"

"Where you at?"

"We went on route. We hit up RBK, now we're at Jillians getting it in on the green. You know how we do."

"So you rode out without me."

"Imani you wanted to do you."

"What time are you coming home?"

"I don't know. I got some runs to make later."

"Later, it's one o' clock."

"I live at night. Why are you all of a sudden tripping?"

"Maybe I wanted to be with you."

"If you wanted to be with me you'd be here. But you had shit to do at ten o' clock on a Saturday night. You call it because I'm not."

I didn't say anything.

"Exactly. Look if I don't see you tonight, I'll meet you at your pops crib for dinner tomorrow."

I hung up the phone and sat in the dark. Being sneaky and conniving only causes complications in love. I feel so disconnected from Quinnzel I may need a calling card to get back. Love may be free but the ceramics cost a grip. The phone rang. I let the machine pick it up.

"Imani pick up the phone," Quinnzel said through the speaker. "I don't know what the deal is and I can't read minds. I know you hear me nigga."

I don't know what to say to him but I picked up the phone anyway.

"Quinnzel, I need you."

"I'm coming."

That's what's up, he didn't ask any questions. Quinnzel came home and we made love like a quiet storm. It was the bomb diggity shot but nothing's changed. I'm still on my grind. Quinnzel got up to make his moves.

"Don't go babe," I said sitting up.

"Imani what's wrong?"

"You are the only thing real to me."

"What?"

"Quinnzel, please just hold me."

He took his clothes off and got back in the bed. Quinnzel wrapped his arms around me.

"Imani you're not saying anything."

"I'm trying to find the words."

"Say what you feel."

"I never want to lose you."

Quinnzel held me tighter and kissed my forehead.

"Nothing is going to happen to me."

"You can't promise me that."

"I can promise you I'ma take good care of you."

"What?" He laughed.

"Imani, I give you all my heart can give. I can't stop loving you."

Quinnzel kissed me and I fell in love with him all over again. His love is what I cry for.

"I love me some you," I said. "I crave you Quinnzel."

"I'm yours all day and don't you forget it."

I kissed his neck.

"Go handle your business, babe."

"Word."

"No. But you have to do what you have to do."

"True." Quinnzel got up and put his clothes on. "We'll holla at some breakfast when I come back."

"Be safe, babe."

"You know it. No worries."

"I love you."

"The word for how much I love you has never been spoken. Get some sleep."

I heard Quinnzel's car pull out of the lot. I closed my eyes but was not graced with sleep. My mind is flooded with unnecessary thoughts of Joey. I can't let him get the best of me. I have to be confident with my shit when I step to him. Body language is a must when being a seductress. His eyes will tell all before he says a word. And eyes don't lie; they reveal true feeling whether you want them to or not. Many a nigga gets caught up for an inviting glance in a damsel's direction. We do have the tendency to confuse looks of lust for love but the eye contact is always the initial reading. I'll get Joey to confide in me once I show him what I'm working with. Two shakes of the bu-dunc-a-dunc-dunc, a twist of the hips, and a pump in the bump-young bull will be begging to drink my bath water.

At dinner Sunday night Dad hit us with some shit. He said he and Mrs. Ilene are going to recite wedding vows. I'm actually cool with it. Everyone deserves someone to love. And if you are fortunate enough to have loved and lost and find love again, no one should stand in the way. I know my dad loves my mom and no one will ever take her place in his heart. But there may be room for one more. Sounds real familiar, Terrell to Quinnzel. The more things change the more they stay the same. I never stopped loving Terrell but Quinnzel has definitely left an impression on me, in me, and around me. And in this big bad world every thing happens for a reason. At that critical moment the reason may be far fetched but please believe the means are crucial. When you figure it out and the jones comes down, things in the game done changed. Quinnzel drove back to my house after dinner. He got in the shower and I did what I have been dreading all weekend.

"Hey Joey, what the deal," I said into the phone.

Quinnzell Supreme Sharpe

Joey kicked some bullshit like he wants me to cause mayhem on a couple of sets to keep 5-0 occupied. I came at him like nigga why don't I just help you make your move, fuck the dumb shit. Dude was on some, I don't get down with you like that. I'm like it's a secret society all we ask is trust. Joey knows I'm all about that dough since I was a day old. That's what niggas trust me to do, get money. I use that to my advantage. He thinks I'm down for the paper and to make sure Derek disappears. That's what's up. I'm riding till the wheels fall off. I'm a catch dude slipping and it's on. Malik got lookouts at Joey's moms' crib just in case. I got Rahiem finding out who posted Derek's bail. Thomas and Williams put the body on ice. If I can get one of their guns, it's over. But I'm a play my part until I can drop the bomb on all them niggas. The team is setting up some major ill shit. My whole clique is the truth, yamean. We got eyes on the hotel to see who's coming and going out of the room. Joey doesn't stay there and he always comes back in a different whip. De is finding out where he parks the other wheels. When it's on, it's on. We're keeping the block shut down until we settle the dust. I met the niggas at the Palace to see what's goings on.

"What's the deal Money?"

"What up Q?" De gave me a pound.

"You just missed Lik. Yo, that nigga is a mastermind. He got shit pumping."

"Word?"

"Feel me," De said counting stacks. "Check this out. Some broad named Asia paid Derek's bond. I got Tiana pulling her cards."

"Tiana?"

"Yeah. She's a hood rat, she don't give a fuck. Asia lives out Chester. I copped Tiana a squatter and she's out there."

"For what?" I sat on the couch.

"To smack home-girl up and leave her sizzling. Find out what she knows and if it's a back draft, let her know it's off with her head."

"And Tiana's your pimpstress."

"Why not, she ain't new to this." De smiled. "Oh yeah. She did tell me y'all have some unfinished business."

"Fuck that smut."

"That's exactly what she wants you to do," De said. He lit a Dutch. "She wants you bad, watch that shit Q."

"You put her ass on."

"This shit is business, y'all hold the personals."

"If it ain't one thing it's a muthfucking nother."

"Word. But scared money don't make money."

"Ain't scared, never scared."

"Makes sense, now make dollars." De gave me a pound. "Yo Q fuck that bitch for real. She can't do shit you don't let her ass do."

He passed me a Corona and I downed that shit. I sat there getting blazed.

"What Lik up to?" I started choking.

"Cough that shit out dude," De said. "He's getting our navy ready to hijack the van after the niggas pick up Joey's cartel from the docks."

"What it's hitting for?"

"The shit is coming from Cuba so if you know like I know it's whatever."

I nodded my head.

"Basic shit."

"So take this run with me right quick."

"Where we out to?"

"Deluxe. I told Tiana to meet us there."

"Let's be out."

We got to Deluxe at ten thirty. Tiana was waiting for us in a booth.

"What's good T," De said.

"Dig the move," Tiana said. "Home-girl didn't know Derek but she used to be Thomas' bitch. He gave her the dough and some dick, she made moves."

"That's good money," De said. He lit a cigarette. "What else?"

"They do be crashing at her spot."

"That could be where Joey stash the whips De," I said

"What you say Supreme," Tiana said.

She was waiting for me to say something to her. Anytime a female is pressed, she'll assume anything you say is directed towards her.

"Your name ain't De. Damn."

"Why is it like that," Tiana said. She ran her tongue across her lips.

"I'm a hit Malik up and see what it's hitting for," I said to De.

"Supreme I know you hear me talking to you." Tiana started getting loud drawing attention.

"What Tiana?"

"I'm saying I'm trying to get with you."

"I'm good. My lady sexes me crazy."

"That fat bitch ain't got shit on me." I smiled.

"Imani got everything you wish you had." I stood up. "Specifically, me. Yo De I'm a be outside."

I waited for De in the truck. It fucks me up how much females hate on each other. Fuck that. Congratulate Sis if she's putting her thing down. Because hating ain't shit but insecurity. See Imani is the type of female who's self-assured; she's confident and secure. So no matter what other female is doing her thing Imani can give props because Sis ain't taking shit away from her. But when you're insecure like Tiana every chick, who looks better, dresses better, whatever becomes an automatic threat. She's your enemy because she got it going on. That shit is ass backwards. If Sis got it going on and you want it like she got it then get with her. Don't come at her neck all crazy giving her the grizzly when she walk pass when you really like her shoes. She could put you on to some shit. I'm a write a book called Uplifting Thy Sistah in the Hood. Fuck that, a nigga is versatile. I got gifts. I laughed at my crazy thinking.

De came outside and got behind the wheel. We went back to the Palace. De went around to the office, I went inside. I walked over to the bar and told Tammy to send a bottle of Cristal up to my table. I went upstairs to VIP and kicked back. Imani came in decked out in a banging ass red dress with her stomach out flexing and her wig all tossed up. I peeped niggas trying to crack on her in the elevator. Of course they got no play. She walked over to my table and stood like the eighth, ninth, and muthfucking tenth wonders of my world.

"You look hot." I stuck my tongue out like a snake.

"Excuse me do I know you?"

I licked my lips.

"Nah, but you need to."

"Why do you say that?"

"So I can show you just how deep love can get."

She bit her bottom lip. Damn. Imani's sexy as shit. I got boners from looking at her.

"What makes you think you can handle me," Imani said smiling. I stood up so she could see. "Say no more sexy daddy."

I pulled Imani close and tongued her down. She hugged me and bit my ear. Imani knows all of my spots.

"No one but you can make me feel the way I feel." I rubbed her back and kissed her neck. "Let's get out of here."

"You're the man."

We got on the elevator and went downstairs.

"Supreme."

We stopped walking and I turned around to see Tiana standing in front of me.

"What's up Tiana?"

"So this is your bitch."

Imani looked at me and smiled. She looked at Tiana.

"I take it bald headed skittle dittle has a problem with me."

"Babe, I got this." I stepped in between Imani and Tiana. "What the fuck is wrong with you?"

"Supreme…"

"You ain't got shit to say to me. If it's about business holla at De Money. Anything else, I don't give a fuck. And don't say shit to my lady."

I turned around and grabbed Imani. She waved to Tiana and started laughing. We went outside and waited for Mike to pull up with Imani's wheels. Tiana ran outside and punched Imani in the back of her head. Imani dipped around and came across with the left. I let her fuck Tiana up for a minute. Fuck that. I only let them get it in because Tiana snuck Imani. Otherwise, I wouldn't have let my Queen rumble, but nobody likes to get stole. I know Imani wanted to put Tiana in her place and let her know she's one to be respected. Watching her get that shit down turned me on. Tiana gripped Imani's dress. She pulled the straps on her back and her top fell down, but Imani kept boxing. I broke that shit up. Tiana went there with the ghetto smack and picked up a bottle.

"Damn Tiana. Take that L on the chin. Chalk that shit up."

"Fuck you Supreme."

She threw the bottle at me. Imani pushed me behind her. The glass broke at her feet. Double De broke through the crowd and Dezionne wrapped a blanket around Imani.

"Fuck you bitch," Tiana said. "You're going to get yours."

"You just hate me because you ain't me," Imani said. "It ain't about shit. I shake haters off regularly."

I told Dezionne to go to the crib with Imani.

"De, let me holla at your peoples."

Me and De went around back.

"Yo, your bosom got box game," De said. "Bitches probably

think she's sweet because she ain't all loud and raunchy."

"Fuck all that, what's up with your girl?"

"She was working with too many emotions."

"And now."

"Look the broad ain't stupid. She's not going to fuck up the rotation on the business side of things. Tiana knows we don't play those games."

"Alright Money. If she fucks up this move, it's on you."

"It's cool baby boss."

"I hear you talking."

I went upstairs and walked through the club. Tiana was sitting at the bar. I stepped to her.

"What the fuck is your problem?"

"Supreme don't give me that shit. I was waiting for you. You left me hanging."

"For damn near two years, nigga please."

"Oh that's funny to you." Tiana puffed her cigarette. "Did you ever stop to think you meant more to me than just dome?"

"I never made a commitment to you T. We had no ties. And you thought rumbling my girl was going to do what?"

"Make you mine."

Damn. She's really feeling me like that.

"Tiana you are a cool shorty but Imani is my wifey."

She closed her eyes.

"You really don't want me."

"No, I don't. And you should never want a man who doesn't want you."

Tiana put her head down.

"Supreme."

"What's up?"

"I'm not going to hurt the game. I'm still down."

"That's good business. Are we cool?"

"We're cool." Tiana gave me a pound. "And your wifey is cool peoples too."

"Mean left hook."

"Hell yeah."

"Keep your head up T. I'm out."

I jumped in the whip and rolled to Imani's. I gave Dezionne my keys so she could get back to the club. I went in the bedroom.

"You okay?" I asked Imani.

She stood up and dropped her robe. Victoria Secret, spring catalog hot shit. Good God.

"I like the way you handled shit tonight." Imani stood in front of me. "Let's get it on."

You damn right.

Imani

"Your expertise has been requested," Dezionne said walking in my office.

She had a fax in her hand.

"I'm already up to my ass in requests and files and…"

"Nae chill. This is what you've been waiting for. The on-going debate about high-schoolers entering the draft."

"Word. I'm an expert?"

"Please. You know you're the shit Lady NBA."

"Speaking of ladies, I'm still trying to converge the attention span to emphasize the WNBA."

"Lift every voice and sing."

"You damn straight. I have a proposal to increase advertising for the WNBA season and…"

"Imani slow down. You are doing too much."

"You ain't ever lied. Fuck it. Let's close up shop."

I got up from my desk and went to the window.

"You need a hug," Dezionne said laughing. "So what's up?"

"Accept the request." I sat on the couch next to Dezionne. "Comcast Sportsnet is the venue?"

"You know it."

"I'm a need a print out of my schedule for the next two weeks."

"I got you. Now what's up with some eateries?"

"Pizza."

"Deep dish."

"Extra cheese and mushrooms."

"Word up."

Dezionne got up and went to her desk. My two-way started

ringing. It's Quinnzel sending me one thousand kisses. How did he know that was just what I needed? Dezionne buzzed my phone.

"What up?"

"Tasha is out here."

"What?"

I went out front.

"Can I help you Tasha?"

"Don't play nice with me. This isn't a social call."

"So what do you want?"

"I didn't get a chance to say anything before but I know Supreme killed Nino. Oh, Quinnzel right."

"Tasha believe me, I understand the magnitude of your loss but Quinnzel didn't…"

"Shut up. You don't know shit."

Dezionne put her hand up and shook her head.

"Nae," she said. "Tasha look. There is nothing for you here. We have nothing to do with this case. If you have identified a suspect you need to go to the police."

"Both of y'all are bullshit," Tasha said. "And you know what, Supreme is just a puppet being played by De Money."

"What do you want from us Tasha," I said.

"I want the truth."

"Tasha the truth is when you play with fire your ass gets burned," Dezionne said.

"That was real enlightening. Thanks bitch."

"I'm a glass. You're a coaster bitch."

Dezionne came from behind her desk. I stood in the middle.

"Tasha I think you need to bounce," I said.

"Count on seeing me again."

"Yo that bitch is crazy," Dezionne said.

"She's hurting D. She lost her man."

I went back in my office. Dezionne followed me.

"Nae are you okay?"

"I understand her pain, that's all."

"Imani."

"Dez. Damn." I sat on the couch. "They never found the guy who killed Terrell. And everyday my heart bleeds for justice. Too many men are behind bars for crimes they didn't commit. And too many murderers, rapists, and child offenders are walking the streets with the same freedoms as you and me."

"Imani you can't blame yourself."

"Look at Tasha. She's out there trying to put a name to Nino's killer. I didn't do shit for Terrell and when I look at her I think I should have. I don't like to say 'should have'."

"Nae get your mind right before I pop a nine right," Dezionne said. "You paid for Terrell's funeral. You send his mom money. You established yourself in spite of losing your pride and joy when most people would have used that as an excuse to quit. That doesn't mean you care any less. You dealt with your pain the best way you knew how."

Dezionne sat on the couch and put her arm around me.

"I hear you Dez."

"Nae you have to live for the day."

"Another day another struggle."

"It's all fundamentals and basics."

"Represent the A6."

We laughed together.

The rest of the day was less melodramatic. I left the office and went straight to my dad's house. Joey should be here at nine. Yeah, I got him when I hollered and spit. I told him everything he wanted to hear because it sounded good. Niggas do that shit all the time. Talking about, I'm trying to see you like that it's not about pussy. But everytime he hollas at you it's a booty call. Then after he gets the pussy he has to find himself, whatever the fuck that means. Anyway, I got Joey thinking it's all about him. I told him we could make it happen like Butch and Sundance. I know he wants to freak me so I have to invent some creative maneuvers to bypass that shit. I'm trying to bring Joey down by any means necessary. But I don't want the means to be my lips,

my hips, my coochie, and my tits. It's bad enough I'm giving this
nigga Quinnzel's quality time. And as much as my boo likes to
be up under me, I know we're about to go through some
changes. Quinnzel is not going to feel this. I need to put some
alibis together until I can get enough evidence to satisfy Jovan's
case and acquit my dude of all suspicions. I may not have captured Terrell's killer but I'm damn sure not going to let Quinnzel
be charged as one. I have to do what's right even though the
wrongs will probably bite me in the ass. I parked behind Amir's
mustang. Of course, I found him in the kitchen.

"What up A?"

"What it look like, Nae?"

"I'm cool." I gave Amir a hug. "You've been missing in
action for a minute."

"I've been putting in work," Amir said. "And getting my
head right."

"Jovan?"

He shrugged.

"Small thing to a giant."

"Amir, I know she fucked up but that doesn't mean she didn't
care."

"What is this, the Jamie Kennedy Experiment? When did you
become Jovan's representative?"

"I'm not repping Jovan. But I do know heart break when I
see it."

"Nae, she played me."

"Everybody plays the fool sometime baby boy. What matters
is what you do after that."

"I can't front Nae, she put me on my ass. I broke out the
Sade collection; you know she makes a nigga want to slit his
wrists."

"There's love in that," I said smiling. "Why don't you hit her
up?"

"It's cool. I got a set of twins giving me some sexual heal-
ing."

"There is a difference between sex and love. I know you know that."

"But pussy and dick are one in the same."

"Spoken like a true nigga who ain't shit."

"That's the plan. I'm too young to have these chickens trying to settle me."

"Do what you feel peoples. I got your back."

"It's only right."

"Where pops at?"

"He and the Mrs. are dining out this evening."

"That's what's up. Well you know what time it is. Bring that ass."

Amir picked up his sandwich.

"You ain't said nothing but a word."

Me and Amir went in the den and I broke his ankles in NBA Live 2003. Somebody's bass started vibrating the windows. I looked at my watch. Eight fifty, it's time to get live. I went outside and met Joey at his car.

"I'm driving." He smiled.

"You got it ma."

I told Amir to stay here until I got back, and jetted before I had to answer his questions. I jumped in my Dad's Lincoln Town Car and drove around front. Joey got in and I rode down to M & Erie to Erie Lanes. Joey set the board up and bowled the first frame.

"So what I got to do to get with you ma," Joey said after his spare.

"Keep it good and plenty."

I hit a strike and no doubt the turkey came next.

"What's that?"

"Keep it real, fresh, and exciting," I said licking my lips.

It's all game. Dude is weak. I shouldn't have to tell him to keep shit on the up and up. Nobody wants a boring ass mate. I wish I were here with my dude instead of this scrub in training. I didn't have to take Quinnzel to love school, he knows how to please and keep me satisfied. And he keeps it right on a daily basis.

"What's up with that sweet, that nasty, that gushy stuff," Joey said squeezing my ass. I'm totally disgusted.

"You're not ready yet."

"Fuck is that supposed to mean man?"

Joey backed up and stared me down. Damn. He's housing a lot of aggression.

"We can get it in when you show me what you're working with."

"You want me to pull my dick out?"

"Don't be broadcasting my shit," I said leaning up against him. "This is me all up in here, remember that."

"You got me like you got me. I'm up."

I killed Joey with my bowl game 210 to 97. He walked out to the car feeling some type of way. I opened the door for Joey and went around to the trunk to get my pocketbook. I checked my two-way. Damn, Quinnzel paged me six times. Not good. Very bad. I put my hand up to close the trunk and somebody grabbed my arm.

"What the fuck." I turned around. "Malik what up?"

Oh shit, how much did he see?

"What's popping Imani? Who that in the car?" he asked. "Is that Q, I got to holla at him."

"Nah that's my dog."

He looked through the glass.

"Looks like you're creeping to me."

"You don't know what you're talking about." I slammed the trunk.

"Word. You right. Be safe Nae. One."

He turned around to walk away.

"Imani."

"Speak."

"Tell Q I said holla at his boy."

Quinnzell Supreme Sharpe

Imani's been getting it in crazy on the grinding tip. I ain't mad, stack that cheese. But take care of home. Never fuck up the vibe at the crib, feel me. I'm not taking it there but what one lady ain't doing, another female will, swell and with the quicks. Hell no, I'm not stepping out on my lady. I'm a one Imani dude. I love her more than she'll ever know. It's just lately shit ain't like it used to be. I'm playing my part, but Imani's not around long enough to experience the magic. That's bad business. I'm only one man. Shit, thugs need hugs too. Once this last move is complete, I'm taking her up out of here for a minute, yamean. Just me and her on some exclusive shit. It doesn't matter where we go as long as Imani is the flight of the navigator. It's the only way to fly.

"Get ya hands off me." I spun around and dropped the fade away jumper in De's grill. "And one."

"No foul, that was all ball."

"Nigga that was wrist and arm but the skills laced nothing but the bottom of the net regardless."

"Man, I went straight up and down."

"Your defense is suspect. Where your game at?"

"Whatever. Check."

"Get yours."

De cut me up with his sweet ass crossover, but I met him above the rim for the rejection.

"Get that weak shit the fuck out of here."

De brought the ball in. I got him with a steal and hit the spot up three ball.

"Game."

"Run it back."

"As soon as you graduate flight school," I said laughing. "Sike nah what's up Money I see you going through something."

"Me and Dezionne went through some shit last night."

"Word, what's up?"

"She's smelling herself trying to see how much shit I'll take off her. I told her ass don't start something she's going to be scared to finish because she can't control the outcome."

"What happened my nigga?"

"Some dude called her moms crib on a late night and shit. And you know Mrs. Bonnie's instigating ass brought the phone in the room drawing for real."

"Who the fuck is dude?"

"Fuck dude, he ain't my girl. He's going to be a man and do what he does. Dezionne know fucking better."

"What she say?"

"She don't know how he got the number. Don't she know that's chapter three, line twenty-six of the pimp textbook. Shit, I wrote the book I ain't the fuck slow."

"What's it going to be?"

"Ain't shit set in stone. And one thing for certain two things for sure, I'm not keeping anybody who doesn't want to be kept."

"It's not that serious Money."

"Nigga I claim Dez what the fuck you mean? But she ain't going to put me out there like I'm a fucking nut. If this ain't where she wants to be, fuck it move on."

I shock my head. You can be a gangster and a gentleman but wifey can't be a ho and a housewife. That's the rules.

"I'm saying you think she's fucking outside of the union?"

"Why is water wet?"

"Why ask why?"

"Exactly. But I haven't been putting in no work or spending no time. I need to check my shit too."

"Work it out."

"Feel me. I love Dez too much to have another nigga up in

my sweet spot."

"I heard that. What you going to do about it?"

"Smack it up, flip it, and make it mo better."

"Do the damn thing. Finesse that ass. Show her something she ain't ever seen before."

"Nigga romance is my stage name."

"Pop your collar pimp daddy."

"You think I didn't when I did."

I picked up my shirt and two-way off of the ground and walked to the back steps of the crib.

"Yo Q what's up with my re-match?"

"Nigga Dezionne already got you whipped. You can't run with me. It's embarrassing. You can't hang."

"Hah. You should be on Def Jam Comedy."

"That's what they tell me."

I went in the crib and took a shower. I got dressed and me and De bust a grub. We rolled to Philly like four o' clock. I went to Miracle Media but Dezionne said Imani had to make a guest appearance at a reading workshop for the read to achieve program sponsored by the NBA.

"Imani's doing big things ain't she Dez?"

"She always does or don't you notice?"

"Dez, I stay up on what my wifey is in to. Please believe me."

"Good. Most niggas don't."

"I'm not most niggas. What's up with all the tension coming from my left?"

"I'm just saying appreciate what you have while you got it because you'll miss it when it's gone."

"Ease back Oprah. I know the specialty I'm working with and I maintain my love's happiness. Can you say the same?"

"I could if he'd let me."

"My analysis is this; the problem is miscommunication the anecdote- get that shit in early on all levels."

Dezionne smiled.

"Sure you right."

"I know I'm right."

"Yeah, well love doesn't love nobody. Make sure you tell Imani you love her everyday."

"It's only right."

"It's the EX factor, trust. Don't learn the hard way."

"I'm on it." I gave Dezionne a hug. "Let's get out of here."

"I got to politic for a minute and get these scouting reports finalized for the agent up and coming in the game."

"Alright I'm a get back. Keep your head up Dez."

"All day. Tell my man to get with me."

"Tell him yourself," De said walking in.

I left Double De to mend their wounds and silence their woes. I rolled to the Palace to chill out and count the Benjamins. Everything else is on freeze until the drop off next week creates a new epidemic. I poured a drink and sat at the desk. Malik came in.

"What's really good with you 'Lik?"

"What the deal Supreme?"

I gave Malik a pound.

"I'm maintaining."

"Yeah. Yo niggas are ready for combat waiting for command."

"That's good money."

"Here's something you might not find so slick."

"Talk to me."

"Imani's dipping out on you."

"Fuck you talking about?"

"She was with Joey up Erie lanes."

"Nah, you tripping."

"Q you know how I get down, come on dog. I ain't got to lie to you for shit. I know how niggas be acting out here about their girls. I'm looking out for you."

"What the fuck man?"

"Yo, I call you my nigga because I got love for you. Handle

yourself but keep Joey at arms length. That nigga is going to get his in a minute. He's going to feel all of the consequences and repercussions."

"Yo nigga show and prove."

"What?"

"When was this?"

"Look nigga I'm not playing house with y'all. You know your shorty and you know when shit ain't right."

"And right now shit ain't right."

"That's my word. You do the math."

I gave Malik a pound.

"Good looking out, yo for real."

"No doubt. I'm out though. Time is money."

"Be safe 'Lik."

"True. I'm a hit you up. One."

"One."

I don't know what to say about this shit. Malik ain't just going to talk out of his ass. And Imani has been distant for a minute. I'm saying, I would rather leave than to cheat. I know Imani ain't go out like that. That's some disrespectful shit. I got something for her ass. I'm a kill her with kindness, make her ass sweat. I paged Imani and told her to be home at nine. She hit me back and said certainly. I went to her crib and cleaned that shit up spic, span, and spotless. I threw down in the kitchen with some lobster tails, jumbo shrimp, king crab legs, and salmon steak. I lit candles and turned on the smooth jazz collection. I took a shower and threw on Imani's favorite soft blue Versace suit with the matching gators. I popped a bottle of Merlot and waited for the sparks to fly. At ten o' clock I paged her and got no response. This is bullshit. At eleven o' clock I blew out the candles and loaded my clip. Somebody's going to feel this wrath. At twelve-thirty I dried my tears and rolled the fuck out. Where do broken hearts go?

Imani

I sat in my seat thinking about Thursday night and its playoff ball. I'll be on the panel with Ernie Johnson and Kenny 'the Jet' Smith for Inside the NBA and two half time shows. I say two half time shows. Boom. It's about to be crazy off the hook in the ATL like its'03 NBA All-Star weekend. You know we getting wild for the night. It's necessary. I've been concentrating so hard on my MacGyver role with Joey it's a wonder I can make a move this big. Consequently, I got two weeks to call this Joey shit a done deal. The hard part is over. I already planted the taps in his car and his crib. And I left a button camera in his car to get footage on who he gets down with. Now we sit back and wait for him to give himself up by clucking like a kitchen bitch. Dezionne buzzed my phone.

"Mommy's on line two."

"Whose mom?"

"Quinnzel's. OOOOHHHH you in trouble," Dezionne said laughing. "And KG the kid, if you seen him with a basketball you know that he grown, called while you were out. He wants to know if you'll do a cameo in his next commercial."

"Can Vince Carter slam dunk?"

"Half man, half amazing. How your funky ass get down with Kevin Garnett?"

"I'm sickening baby. And his sneakers are And1. Get get yours."

"The girl is poposterious."

"Set it up. Let me take this call. Hello."

"Hey pretty face."

"Hi Mrs. Ayana."

"Girl didn't I tell you to call me Mommy A. Ain't nobody above an ass whipping now."

"Yes ma'am."

"That's the same mess I had to tell Mr. Quinnzel Zyhid last night."

"Zyhid? Q told me he didn't have a middle name."

"Imani, Zyhid was Quinnzel's first name. He was named after his dad. As you can imagine Q is not too fond of his father so he abandoned the name. Told everybody he was his own man not Zyhid's man."

"Yikes. Sounds complicated."

"Quinnzel is determined to be the dad his wasn't." She sighed. "He's bearing a weight on his shoulders. He sounds unsure of himself. What's going on?"

"I'm not sure."

"You're supposed to take care of your man, girl. Or are you too wrapped up in your own activity."

"I have been preoccupied lately."

"No no Imani. Keep your man happy. Didn't you learn anything from the Queens of Comedy?"

I laughed.

"Imani you need to comfort your man and find out what's troubling him."

"If it's street ties he won't tell me."

"I'm going to tell you like I told Dezionne, get your man out of those streets."

"I can't make him do something he doesn't want to do."

"Imani you are a woman honey, a beautiful black butterfly. You can excel doing whatever you put your mind to. Make him an offer he can't refuse girl."

"How?"

"I can't tell you how or what to say. It has to come from your heart, that's the only way you'll connect with his."

"Sounds logical. Can I make it happen?"

"Q has to know you have his best interest and the greatest of

intentions in mind and at heart. Be honest; don't make it seem as
if you have an ulterior motive."

"I don't want to go there Mommy A. I can't cry those tears."

"You'd rather cry mournful tears?"

"No."

"Imani I said all of this to you because you are not a dumb
ass chicken head from the street. My son is just playing with.
You are Quinnzel's marrying maiden; I believe that in my heart.
He celebrates your love.

I heard her crying.

"Save him please. Together you will get through the storm."

"I will."

"And bring me some grand babies."

"Yes ma'am."

"Imani don't be afraid. My son holds you dear. I'm sure you
know that."

"I do. Thank you for having so much faith in us."

"As long as you two love each other, God will see you
through."

"True love is a blessing."

"Just keep doing what you're doing pretty face. Mommy A
loves you."

"Imani loves Mommy A too."

"Well Imani better pick up the phone more often and act like
she knows."

"I will."

"Anytime Imani, about anything."

"Definitely."

"I'll speak to you later."

"Peace."

Damn. I didn't know she was riding for me. When we had
girl talk, she shared secrets with me. And coming from his
moms' lips to my ears, I love it.

I went on route to my house for lunch. I took my shoes off
and went in my bedroom. I watched Quinnzel sleeping, breathing

deeply. So tranquil and quiet. I wish I could steal all of his worries and free his mind. I damn sure would if I could. I give all of myself to Quinnzel. The sun doesn't shine without him. I blew Quinnzel a kiss and went in the living room. I sat on the couch and knocked his jacket on the floor. I picked it up and a key card fell out of his pocket. The DoubleTree Hotel. Why is Quinnzel staying at a hotel? I put the card in my briefcase. Damn that. If Quinnzel is creeping his ass just got caught up. But I'm a do some investigating before I draw any conclusions. I'll give him the benefit of the doubt no problem. I've never had a reason to suspect Q has been cheating. But I have been doing my own thing as of late. Niggas get lonely. Hold Nae, I'm thinking too much. I put my shoes on and went back to the office. Damn, now I'm bugging. I let that girl Tiana enter my thoughts and I feel some type of way. She did the same shit Jovan did. And unless her ass is national security shit is about to get hectic. I tried to focus on basketball with nothing doing. Fuck it. I'm a come at his neck, this ain't a fucking game. Just like he checked my two-way and got Derek's number is the same way the DoubleTree is the topic of discussion. Females forgive but we never forget. I picked up the phone to call my house but Dezionne walked in my office. I don't need her cosigning my madness, yet. I hung up the phone.

"What up Dez?"

"Nae, I am not feeling it right now."

"What's wrong?"

"It could be the flu with the weather changing."

"Keep your germs to yourself contaminated ass. Go home."

"Love is contagious, it's alright. Give me a hug."

"I will drop you where you stand. Get the hell on. Call me later."

"I'm out. Smooches."

Dezionne left and I picked up where I left off. Before Quinnzel could answer the phone my other line lit up. Shit.

"Thank you for calling Miracle Media."

"Ms. Best please."

"This is she. May I ask who's speaking?"

"It's Price."

"What's up Jovan?"

"I have some information that may be the missing link we need. Thanks to you."

"That's what's up. What you got?"

"There's a car waiting for you outside."

Quinnzell Supreme Sharpe

Me and Imani are off centre. Left knows not what right is doing. My heart is torn like a muthafucka. My miz kicked some shit like if I hugged Imani as tight as I hugged the block she couldn't stray. But fuck that. I ain't giving her no dirty dick so she can't come at me with no ran through pussy. I'm waiting to see what bullshit she spit to deny this shit. I pulled up to Mr. Darren's crib drunk as shit on some early morning shit. I got out the whip and shit got ugly. Joey walked up to me.

"So tell me does absence make the heart grow fonder," he said smiling.

"What the fuck are you doing here?"

"Looking for my bitch. But I'm beginning to think she doesn't really live here."

"Your bitch?"

"Yeah big booty ho, nigga you know you love her."

"Imani is…"

"Not of importance if you know what time it is."

"Nigga what?"

"Money over bitches' nigga stick to the script. Thursday night, shipment, handle business or you know the rest. Holla, swallow, for a dollar. I'm out."

I reached for my gat. Don't blow the plan Supreme. I released myself.

"You got it J, its butter."

I ain't even go holla at Mr. D. I jumped in the whip and rolled straight to Miracle Media. I'm a crack Imani's muthafucking forehead. I bumrushed her in her office.

"Imani cut the shit. What the fuck is up with you and that

nigga Joey?"

She stood up to me.

"I'm trying to save your life."

"What the fuck are you talking about?"

Imani held her ground.

"Quinnzel don't give me that shit. You live on the block and I'm riding for you for sure."

"What's up with you and that nigga then?"

"I'm undercover."

"You 5-0?"

"Something like that. But Jovan is coming for Joey's head not yours."

"Jovan?"

"Yes babe. It's not about you. And please believe me I didn't do nothing with him."

"So what you got?"

"Cameras and taps in his car. What you know about that?"

I smiled.

"Yo, Jovan is your partner in crime. I ain't telling you shit dog."

"I'm a grown ass woman. You have to trust that I'm holding you down. Damn Q, I don't remember asking you for shit. Why won't you give yourself to me?"

"I am. Imani I was born the day you loved me. But…"

"No buts. Either you want me or you don't."

"You know I want you. I need you."

She nodded her head.

"Babe, I'm not apologizing because I didn't do anything wrong. I'm ready, willing, and able by your side. Let me show you."

"You just did."

I kissed Imani like I never kissed her and our love started over. I hugged her and clutched her shoulders.

"Quinnzel what are you afraid of?"

"Let me be a man, Imani. I can't have you out there like that.

You have to understand where I'm coming from."

"I do, babe."

"Imani." I looked her in her eyes. "You are my future. Please I'm asking you to tell Jovan you're finished."

"Anything for you babe." She kissed me. "It's done."

"Bet that. Thank you for being woman enough to do what you did."

"You know I'm dangerous."

"True. But you're done romancing the stone."

"Only you boo."

"Just us Love."

Imani wiped my tears.

"You had me about to lose my mind."

"I had the greatest of intentions at heart."

"That's what we live for. But promise me this."

"What's that?"

"You'll love me and only me forever and a day."

"As long as you'll have me."

Dezionne buzzed the phone.

"Imani your eight o' clock is here."

"Give me a minute Dez."

"It's cool. Handle your shit," I told her.

"Will I see you at home?"

"You better believe it. I'm a ball your ass up."

Imani kissed me.

"I love you babe."

"Me too. Maybe too much."

"I deserve all of it. Don't deny what you feel."

"You damn sure do in more ways than one. You will always be my baby. I'm a get at you."

Imani hugged me and didn't want to let me go.

"Come on. You got people waiting on you."

"You are all that matters."

"Let me find out Imani's ready to settle." I raised an eyebrow.

"I just may be so Q better be careful what he asks for."

"I just might get it huh."

"Ain't nothing wrong with that."

"I heard that. What you think about you, me, candles, roses, whipped cream, and strawberries."

"You know I like that freaky shit."

I blew Imani a kiss and rode to the Palace. Yeah my lady is a muthafucking cannon. She was getting down for the Bull. Imani; I thank God for her, yamean. Beside every strong man is a bullet-proof woman tougher than nails. All I need in this life of sin is me and my down ass woman. Time to check niggas status and the whole nine. I went to the office to holla at De.

"Yo Money shit is vertical."

"What you mean my nigga?"

I sat next to De on the couch.

"The cops definitely want Joey, so we got to get that nigga first."

"Everything is everything. Thursday night it's on."

"Holla at Rahiem. See if he can trace a tap planted in Joey's car."

"How the fuck a tap…"

"Don't ask niggas, show and tell. Get a location on dude."

"Bet. Rahiem will hold us down."

"True. See what he can get on Jovan too."

"Jovan?"

"Yeah. Operation dummy mission."

"I got you. Oh, check it. Malik went to pick that shit up from Monster."

"Word. He got a stash?" De nodded.

"Yup, he's low key. It's going to be wild for the night."

"Bring it."

"Ain't shit to it but to do it."

"Yo, you and Dez bridge that gap."

"Hell yeah, hell yeah. She was feeling neglected and shit wearing her heart on her sleeve. I regulated."

"That's what's up."

"Ain't nothing. But uh let me make these moves."

"I'll see you."

De gave me a pound and rolled. I did inventory and stocked up the bar. I took some loot to the bank and went downtown. I copped a couple pairs of timbs and some fresh RocaWear and Polo gear. I went to pick up some earrings for Imani but wound up peeping out engagement rings. I'm in that zone. And from the soul of a man, on a day like this, I'm trying to make it. Imani deserves to be happy so I'm a break my back to please her. I'm ready to learn. Momma said there would be a day like this and I'm feeling it. I've been feeling it. Imani asked me what I'm afraid of. I'm afraid of losing her. A nigga like me will fuck up without knowing. I don't want to be that stupid. I'm rendered defenseless with Imani. I yield to her emotionally. If she ever said she was out I would be no more good. I need to reassure her that my feelings are unconditional. And to my understanding she's all I want and need. I don't have to convince myself, I need to commit myself devoutly. Imani is the one. I knew that the first time I laid eyes on her when she walked into O'Hara's. I felt it. And every time I see her face I know even more. Imani is the one to get me out the streets.

I drove around for a minute getting my shit together. I met De back at the Palace at five o' clock. He ain't have shit good to say. Rahiem can't touch Jovan. We got to play this one by ear. He said he'd holla back on the tap he might be able to trace it freestyle. What the fuck ever. I told De to do what he do and went to be with my lady. I opened the door and heard Imani singing, 'You turned my whole world around'. I went in the bedroom. Imani sat on the bed like a dream come true painting her toenails, smelling like lick me all over. She got up when she saw me.

"What's up?"

Imani hugged me and took my jacket off.

I smiled at her.

"What's up, sexy?"

Imani kissed me.

"Your dinner is in the oven. I'll go heat it up."

I grabbed Imani's hand before she could leave the room.

"Sit down," I announced.

Imani sat on the bed. I sat on the floor beneath her. I put her foot in my lap and picked up the nail polish from the night table. Imani looked down at me. Something in her eyes captured my soul. I painted her toenails, while she smiled a wide smile.

Imani

How do you know if your man really loves you? It's in his kiss and his touch. His love lives in his eyes with every look in yours. It's more than saying those three words. I need action from a man, you know. Love is an expedition through time that can't be erased. A journey that makes your bond stronger. Intertwined hearts accent a sacred union. I used to get my swerve on early back in the day. Cierra, and me we used to kill the block before I met Terrell. And it wasn't shit out there for me but a lot of empty fucking. Blessing in the lesson: don't open your legs for every man who throws his dick at you. It could be some hot shit in the mix too, case and point. Please believe me. Quinnzel, a real love, brings so much more. When you find the same you'll know the oneness I'm talking about. And you'll never want to let it go. Please believe me. It's that Clare and Cliff, Jada and Will, my Aunt Terri and Uncle Joey romance. No doubt you're going to go through dumb shit but when you and your boo can go through it crazy and still all you want is each other you know it's for real. Only real love can triumph over the hell of ordeals. Nothing else can compare to the colors of love. Have faith; love each other for who you are.

And to my ladies I know we sometimes give more than we get but damn that. He has to need you. If he only wants you, he can find that same want in another. Needing is indefinite it can't be secondary. So let us stop settling for every Tom, Dick, Harry, and Craig and them. Because if you don't stand for something you'll fall for anything.

I woke up to breakfast in bed with Quinnzel as the delicacy. He is the truth like Sojourner. Mandingo in the sack. I like it. I like it. I went to work with a Kool-Aid smile like no other.

"You look revived, rejuvenated, and revitalized home skillet," Dezionne said.

When you are completely happy it radiates to a glow. I am definitely beaming.

"You know we got it like that Dez."

"Do your thing. I am not mad at you girl."

"Me and Q are in a zone. I'm loving it and I'm making it a priority to stay this way."

"Hush your mouth. No you didn't just say the P-word."

"Yes I did. Slowly, but surely I'm a make it happen."

"I'm scared of you. Let me find out."

"Imani Heaven Sharpe representing."

"It's good to be the best but it's better to be sharp."

"I know that's right. I'm ready to learn."

"You go girl."

"Thank you girl. Boom. Let's make some money."

Dezionne got up and walked to the door. The phone rang.

"I got it Dez. Good morning Miracle Media. This is Imani."

"Imani, it's Price."

"Hi Jovan."

"You've been fleeing from me Imani. What's going on?"

"I'm out."

"What? Imani I'm close. Work with me on this."

"Jovan listen. My family comes first, second, and third in my life. And being caught up with you is hurting them. I can't do it."

"What about Terrell Davis?"

"That was a low blow Jovan. I see you're getting down and dirty. Well you can kiss…"

"Imani, I'm not trying to play you. I think his murder may be avenged here."

"I'm listening."

"I pulled the file, it's incomplete. Cartilage casings but no gun was recovered is the reason why no one was convicted."

"And? Tell me something I don't know."

"Terrell dealt in heavy drug traffic."

"Jovan…"

"Imani, Terrell was murdered for something he saw or something he knew. It was a professional hit. And the police report has more than its share of discrepancies."

"Meaning?"

"Damn it. Can't you read between the lines?"

"I prefer the lines actually. Be specific with yours."

"Dirty cops Imani. I'm on to something. Please give me more time. I'll show you."

"Jovan do what you do. I wish you well and I hope you crack this shit. Terrell's death should not be in vain. But I can't be down."

"Imani please reconsider."

"You don't need my help you can do this. You have to. It's what you do and I think you're damn good."

"If you're not careful I might start to think you care."

"I do care Jovan. Good luck Detective."

"Coming from you it means a lot. I'll get the bastard."

"Head on a platter."

"I'll keep you informed."

"Take care of yourself out there Jovan. Be safe. Peace."

I hung up the phone feeling real good about exchanging pleasantries with Jovan. I already make more enemies than friends. It's nice to know I can overcome bullshit and move on. There is no need for bad karma. Dezionne buzzed my phone.

"Your nine o' clock is here."

"Come on back Dez."

This lady has been tackling Dezionne for a month trying to get on my schedule. And I have no idea who she is. But I keep my corporate circle inclined for new prospects. I stood up to meet my guest.

"Ms. Thorne," I said extending my hand. "It's a pleasure."

"Likewise. Please call me Destiny."

"Beautiful name."

"As is yours Imani Heaven."

I smiled.

"I've always liked it. What can I do for you Destiny?"

She shifted in her seat.

"I'm Ilene's daughter."

It seemed like she was going to say something else.

"Okay. You're here for the wedding."

"Yes."

"Cool. Your mom has made my dad the happiest he has been since my mother passed."

"Yeah, our dad has been through a lot. My mom will take care of him."

"Thank you I appreciate that. So are you… Hold. Did you say 'our dad'?"

"Yes. Imani I am your sister."

"What, who, when, where, why, how?????"

"I know it's a bit much. I told daddy I wanted to be the one to tell you."

"Don't call him that."

"Imani your father, our father, has always been a part of my life. And just because you are a selfish spoiled brat that doesn't change anything."

"You don't even know me Ms. Thorne."

"Imani I'm thirty-one so as your older sister I must tell you whining is not attractive or at all becoming of you."

I fixed my face.

"So what's your story?"

"Well, my mom and our daddy were together, until they broke up. He met your mom, fell in love, I was born, and the rest is his story."

"And fate brought my mom and our dad back together."

"Cinderella couldn't have asked for a happier ending."

"Anything else I need to know?"

"You have grown into a beautiful woman, baby sis."

"You knew me?"

She nodded her head and smiled.

"I always knew you would be a success. From Barbie to your step teams to student government, you had a competitive nature about you. A determination to win and be the best. Quite a child prodigy."

I smiled.

"Imani, I would like a chance to be a part of your life if you'd let me."

"I've always wanted an older sister."

"I'm here."

"Yes you are."

I put my head down.

"What's wrong Nae?"

"How did you know Nae was my nick name?"

"I'm your sister remember."

"I don't believe my dad had another daughter."

"Imani, your mom knew. She didn't want any strife so she wanted to keep us separate until you and Amir were old enough to understand. Your mother was an unbelievable woman."

"Don't I know it?"

"Circumstance kept me away back then you know. But…"

"You're here now."

"Exactly."

"Destiny I would love to know you."

She looked at me with tears forming in her eyes.

"Thank you Imani. I was not expecting you to accept me."

"Why?"

"Thick skin and a tougher skull run in the blood line."

"You are definitely my sister."

Quinnzell Supreme Sharpe

A woman can't change a man. A man has to want to change himself for himself and by himself. To be a better man or a man period. A woman may unveil the path but the man in the mirror has to make the change. And I'm ready to stop being a thug and become a man. A father, a protector, a provider. I know where I want to be and what I have to do to get there. Tonight is my last night as Supreme. It's time for Quinnzel Sharpe to surface and take his place in the circle of life. I'm a make it good for Imani. She more than earned it. I'm getting a crib built with her name on it. I just need the spot. I'm a have a floor designed as her office so she can do business from home. Our house will most definitely be a home. I've been having dreams about that shit. It's time.

I went to the Palace to link up with my niggas. We're going to shake shit up at the docks and it's over. I'm done. Forget everything and everybody. I can't help it if I wanted to.

"Yo, De what up?"

I stood at the bar across from De.

"Rahiem got snagged. His whole shit is under investigation."

"Say word."

"That's my word," De said. "The feds is rushing the docks tonight cousin. They know what's up."

"Niggas are going to come at our necks like we dropped dime or some shit."

"Yo, he must've been running his mouth," Malik said. "Jovan had the whole shit locked with taps and the whole nine."

"I ain't got time for this shit," I said slamming my fists on the bar top. I snapped my fingers. "Thomas and Williams."

"What you thinking," De said.

"If they got the drop on Rahiem those niggas ain't far behind. Let's speed up the process."

"And do what," De said.

"They get a cut off of Joey's shipment tonight right," Malik said.

"For sure," I said. "Charge that to the game. Put them niggas at the crime scene."

"Hell yeah. Two off duty cops at a bust they don't know about how they figure that," De said laughing. He gave me a pound.

"Exactly. Let them snake muthafuckas slither out of this shit," I said. "Damn Derek."

"Oh shit," Malik said. "Yo, his body has to be in the trunk of one of those wheels."

"Joey ain't been pushing that yellow Camero for a minute," De said. "He kept that sweet ass ride on display."

"Flossing hard," I said. "Bet. We got a location on the wheels?"

"Only one place they can be," De said. "Asia's spot."

"Let's be out," Malik said.

We drove out Chester and no doubt the wheels were parked on Asia's acres. She was most receptive to a fifteen grand fee. I felt bad for her so I tossed her another five and told her to get the hell out of dodge. She was way ahead of me because her bags were already packed. Home girl was used all up and finally fed up with the bullshit. She gave up tapers and told us the body was in the Benz. Joey probably figured we'd come for the ride he stopped pushing once we put shit together. Don't trust niggas no farther than you can throw them. Asia gave De the keys and we went out to the field. He popped the trunk and we found every-thing we've been searching for.

We ditched the Benz at Malik's chop shop out in Camden. Check and the fuck mate. Now I got to grease up Jovan. All she got to do is check the slugs. They weren't smart enough to take them out of his chest. Stupid is as stupid does. Offense throws an interception; defense stands tall and forces a fumble. I like the way I think. I hope Thomas and Williams are already on Jovan's shit list. I told the niggas to watch for breaking news and rolled out. I picked up some jerk chicken, cabbage, rice and peas, and plantains for Imani and rolled to her spot. She smiled when she saw me.

"What up babe? I missed you all day."

Imani met me at the door and kissed me. I put my arms around her waist and held her hot body on mine.

"Damn, is it like that?"

"It's always like that."

I kissed Imani and felt the slow grind in her hips. I love the way she freaks me with intensity.

"Imani are these the earrings you…Well hello Quinnzel."

Imani turned around and leaned against me.

"Q this is my sister Destiny."

"What's up Destiny?"

"Imani, I marvel over the company you keep," Destiny said smiling.

"Don't get dropped," Imani said laughing.

I walked in the living room and sat on the couch.

"Baby, I brought you some grub."

I gave her the bag. I damn near forgot about with Imani giving me all the sweetness at the door.

"Thanks babe." Imani sat next to me.

"You come bearing food and you call her Baby," Destiny said. "What is your product code and model type?"

"He's one of a kind and all mines," Imani said.

"I have learned to respect the power of love," Destiny uttered. "Uncharted territory."

"Did I interrupt you two?" I asked the ladies.

"No, we breathe around these parts brother," Destiny said. "But you can tell me what your intentions are with my baby sister."

"Destiny," Imani said. "I'm a big girl now. See all grown up."

"Wipe the simulac off your mouth and shut up."

Imani rolled her eyes at Destiny and pouted her lips.

"I'll give you something to pout about," Destiny said, "Q speak your piece."

"I give Imani all of me," I said. "She's a love I never knew. I'm grateful and appreciative. I'll die giving her the world."

"Babe," Imani said. "I love you boy."

She kissed me and put her legs up on my lap.

"Good answer," Destiny said.

"It's not an answer it's the truth," I said.

"Damn even better," Destiny said. "I wish you two a lifetime of love and happiness. And the way Imani floats, I know your foundation is well established. Keep it tight."

"That's a promise," I said.

Destiny nodded her head.

"Imani cherish what you have girl. And never let a bitch fuck up your home."

Damn she got hostile on that note. She's definitely speaking from experience.

"Destiny, I know what I have," I said. "Twenty females don't measure up to my wifey. She's more than a woman. We don't have those issues."

"Imani is the bomb isn't she," Destiny said.

"You ain't ever lied," I said.

"Alright y'all damn," Imani said.

"Okay sis. I'm a let y'all do what y'all do," Destiny said. "I'll see you at daddy's house tomorrow."

Imani stood up and hugged Destiny. She grabbed her bag and they walked to the door.

"Be safe Destiny. Call me later."

"Shit girl with all of that chocolate my phone would be unplugged at eight o' clock on a nightly basis."

"I know that's right."

"Good night Quinnzel."

"Alright Destiny."

Imani kissed Destiny's cheek and closed the door.

"I see you two are getting down," I said.

Imani smiled.

"I'm glad she's here. And you know what's funny?"

"What's that?"

"It seems as if she has always been here. I feel close to her."

There's a look in Imani's eyes that wasn't there before. Like her heart is whole now.

"You always wanted an older sister didn't you?"

"How did you know that?"

"I know you."

"I bet you do. So do you know what I want right now?"

I got up and stood in front of Imani.

"You want to be close to me."

Imani unbuttoned my shirt.

"I want you to make love to me like love has never been made before."

"Ain't nothing to it but to do it."

I picked Imani up and she wrapped her killer sexy thighs around my waist. She can crush a tennis racket between them things. I carried Imani in the bedroom and laid her on the bed kissing her cotton soft body. She is love. I stirred taffy and felt Imani's soul. She quivered beneath me and cried. We sat up laughing and talking. And Imani finally bust my ass in chess. I got up to take a shower. Imani came in the bathroom and washed my back.

"This is what good love feels like," Imani said.

"The proof is in the pudding and the best is yet to come."

"Tasty love."

"Please believe me."

Imani bit my ass.

"Holla at your girl."

She left the bathroom. Me and Imani spent the night freaking. And the freaks come out at night. Imani slept in Friday morning.

I called Dezionne and told her Imani was running late. She ain't leave the crib until ten o' clock.

"Babe don't forget to be at my dad's house at eight o' clock."

"I'll be there at seven fifty-nine."

"You're an angel."

"I know you're not leaving with my sugar girl."

Imani dropped her briefcase and kissed me the right way at the wrong time.

"Go ahead before I kidnap your ass."

"Promises promises."

I smacked her ass

"I love you , girl."

"I love you more. I'm out."

Imani left and I took a cold shower to chill the fuck out. I can't help it though, Imani's irresistible. I threw on a RocaWear sweat suit to go get a grub. A note was on my windshield: 'tell your sweetie to lock the door.'

Imani

It's a love story. Flowers on pillars, ribbons in the sky. We made the back yard jazzy. Mrs. Ilene is stunning in her periwinkle Donna Karen gown. Destiny and I stood by her side touched to tears. Amir and daddy stood firm like stallions. I looked over at Quinnzel looking right in his Armani tux. He blew me a kiss. I definitely await the privilege of entering the secret garden of marital bliss and spending forever with Q. There's no pressure, I'm patient. I take it all in stride like a big dog. Daddy and Mrs. Ilene recited their own written vows and were pronounced. The wedding party took leave and we got it on. I fixed Quinnzel's plate: turkey, mashed potatoes and gravy, string beans, stuffing, yams, macaroni and cheese, and corn bread. I went to the family table and sat Q's plate in front of him. I sat down in between my dad and Quinnzel.

"Thank you, wifey."

I winked at him and nodded my head. We ate and I got nice drinking hypnotic. We shot the shit talking about the good old days and better new days. Amir was the first to break the cipher at eleven o' clock talking about it's time to go get jiggy with it. The guests had already begun to scatter. DeShawn and Dezionne left too. I hugged and kissed my dad and his bride and said good night.

I held Quinnzel's hand on the drive to my house. He put my hand to his lips and gave it a French kiss. I rubbed his head and closed my eyes. With Q by my side all of my wishes come true. He's someone I can call my own. Now I'm feeling real freaky. Let's bring this day to a pleasant close. We got personal and a bit freak nasty and made honey love on the balcony. How ill is that to get physical under the stars upon heights? Holla back Juliet you ain't got shit on me darling. Q is rhyme and reason, a cherished song worth singing. On the strength of who he is, he gets home-style loving from the bottom to the top. I make his body shake and shudder with zesty, spicy loving jumping with flavor. I keep Quinnzel intrigued and wanting more. Erotica sends him on quests for more treats. And reciprocated pleasure is a reward all in itself. Please believe me.

"I keep falling in love with you," Quinnzel said shivering.

I kissed his lips.

"What you don't know."

He wrapped the blanket around us and we went inside. I put my robe on and Quinnzel went in the kitchen. I snatched the blanket off his ass and ran in the bedroom. I had candles lit and music playing before he came in. Q and I lay down and I rested with my head on his chest.

"Imani," Quinnzel said. "Your love is like pure ecstasy."

He breathed heavily and rubbed my back. I know he's about to nod out.

"Sleep my love."

"I love you."

I pulled the covers up over our bodies and turned over.

"Come here, girl. I've been waiting all day to hold you."

"You can hold me 24/7."

Quinnzel wrapped me up. His warm body heat seduced me. I slid on top of him and freaked one more ride. This time, even harder.

"You just don't know what you do to me," I said after I came thrice. "I'm still dripping wet."

"I can feel you," Quinnzel said sucking my sweaty breasts. "Don't stop."

"Oh are you trying to sleep in it?"

"You're the best."

We freaked all night. I walked on clouds, danced on rainbows, knocked on Heavens door and said thank you for my starship. Quinnzel takes me there. He tastes good to me. Morning came. I'm dead to the world knocked out. The damn ringing ass phone fucked up the rotation.

"Yes." I didn't even open my eyes.

"Imani it's Price."

"I'm sleep. Call me back yesterday."

"Imani don't hang up."

"What?"

"Derek is dead."

I popped up.

"Oh my God."

"Yes, such tragedy," Jovan said. "His body was found in the trunk of a car."

"Wait a minute; wasn't he supposed to be in jail?"

"A lady named Asia Simms paid his bond. She also paid the price for it."

"Price for what?"

"I don't know yet. But her house was set on fire just before the car was recovered."

"Same device used to blow Dezionne's crib."

"Aren't you smart? Two points for you."

"I stay on my toes. So where does Asia fall into all of this."

"I'll let you know as soon as I get forensics and find out who the car is registered to. Imani hold on."

I heard muffled voices. Damn this is crazy.

"Imani it's our car."

"What?"

"Joey's car," Jovan said hype as shit. "I'm going to review the film from the button cam and call you back."

"Don't forget about me."

"Never that."

"Call me man. Peace."

I hung up the phone and lay back down. Q rolled out about five this morning. Damn, I'm reaching. Fuck it. I'm glad it's the weekend. I went to sleep and got up at one. I took a bath and put on my pink RocaWear sweat suit. I sparked up the grill with hamburgers, sausages, ribs, and chicken. I made some devil eggs and macaroni/tuna salad. The fam should be here by five, six o' clock. All the food is done. The fish and corn were the last two things to come off the grill. I turned the volume up on the Blueprint 2 and grabbed Bacardi Silver. The intercom buzzed.

"Yo."

"Sister."

"Come on up."

Amir and Destiny came upstairs. As soon as I closed the door the buzzer rang again.

"Yeah."

"It's Dez."

I opened the door for Dezionne and went in the kitchen to make my plate. Everybody ate like three times. We bussed up spades and chilled like that. Me and Amir set Destiny and Dezionne back to back.

"It's over," Amir said. "Get it down like a player."

I gave Amir five two times.

"Holla."

"Y'all ain't like that," Destiny said.

"Deal them things again," Dezionne said.

I shuffled the cards and dealt. The door opened and Q, DeShawn, and Malik came in. Quinnzel walked over and kissed me real good.

"What up?" he asked me with his sexy smile.

"Give me more."

Quinnzel laughed and kissed me again.

"Food is in the kitchen babe. I got you."

"Chill. I got it."

DeShawn and Malik were already munching. We played the hand and set them one more time for board.

"Y'all ain't no comp," Amir said.

"Hold youngin you want to romp," DeShawn said. "You want some work?"

"You ain't ready De," I said.

Q and DeShawn looked at each other and cracked up.

"Look out Dez," Quinnzel said. "Sling them things."

They bust our ass twice but we redeemed ourselves on the third game and pulled wheels twice. I looked at the clock. Damn it's one already.

"Yo, y'all ain't got to go home but you got to get the hell out of here," I said standing up.

"Yeah yo, y'all are intruding on my QT," Quinnzel said.

He got up and stood behind me. He kissed my neck and wrapped his arms around my waist.

"Get up on a room," Destiny said.

"You know," Amir said. "Kicking niggas out and shit."

"I got nothing but love for you baby boy," I said. Thanks for cleaning up loser, I mean Destiny."

"Good one. Remind me to beat your ass later. I don't want you and your man to stroll me."

"You know how we do," Quinnzel said.

I gave him a pound.

"Hell yeah babe."

Everybody got their shit together.

"Write me, call me," I said and closed the door behind DeShawn. "Hey you."

"What up beautiful?"

"Why don't you come and see me some time big boy."

I strutted to the bedroom.

"Shake your ass. I know what you're working with."

"Remix."

Today was a good day. Sunday morning Quinnzel had to drive to Maryland. I spent the day at my dad's house helping clean out the basement. I went home on a late night dirty and tired as shit. I parked and walked up the steps to the door of my building.

"Imani."

I blinked and black was the last thing I saw.

Quinnzell Supreme Sharpe

"Young grasshopper," Dezionne said walking up in the office. "Dog, you sexing my girl head off, so she can't get up and come to work in the morning. Especially busy ass Monday."

"I aim to please," I said giving Dezionne a pound. "Hold. Imani ain't go to work today."

I picked up my two-way off the desk.

"I thought you knew."

I paged Imani and sat back. Dude was talking all greasy in that note and shit. I know little nigga ain't that bugged the fuck out his shoes. I hit De on the Nextel walkie-talkie shit. Niggas had to upgrade the technology. I don't really dig bussing up it up on the horn and shit so we got a system. State your destination and arrival.

"Yo meet me at the spot."

"Three minutes," De said.

Imani ain't hit me back yet. I checked the bezel bubble. Seven-thirty damn. I called Imani's crib and got no response.

"She ain't call you Dez?"

"That's what I'm saying. I thought y'all was being y'all and rolled out on some Q spontaneity. You know how y'all do. What's up?"

"Ain't shit."

Dezionne gave me that look and I knew she was about to get started.

"Pump your brakes Dez."

De walked in before she could say shit so now she won't say shit. That's the deal. Right now ain't the time for lectures. I need to know where my wifey is at. Double De got their greet in. De walked up to the desk.

"Excuse me Dez," I said standing up.

She picked up the logs from in front of me.

"Find her."

"Dez…"

"Don't say shit to me. You heard what I said. Ain't shit slow about me."

Dezionne snatched up her bag and hit the door. She cut the corner quick as shit.

"What's popping baby boss?"

De sat on the desk and stared me in my grill. Always look a man in the eye. De does it with authority sonning you and shit. Rather me. Don't mistake it my man intimidates many a nigga. But it has always been his position to look out for me. His brothers' keeper on some really real shit. I took the note out of the desk drawer and put it in De's hand. He opened it.

"Who sent it?"

I ain't say shit.

"Nigga you know who done it." He stood up. "Where?"

"Imani's crib."

"Why ain't you say shit?"

"I don't want you to hold my hand and shit·dog. Not on this one. This nigga Joey is one of my demons God sent here to face me. I'm facing this nigga. Blood in blood out."

"Standing for I."

"Straight up."

Malik beeped in on the phone.

"Yo Money."

"Business."

"Six minutes."

De looked at me

"I got some heat for you my man. I'm a tell you like this, I will rob and steal with you."

"Dog, nigga what."

"Ride til we die." We said that shit together.

I gave my nigga a pound and patted his back. I sat down in the chair.

"What's going on with you," De said.

I picked up the phone and dialed Imani's number one more time. All I got was the machine.

"Imani ain't show up for work today. I don't know what I'm thinking."

"Where her fine ass big booty sister staying at?"

I nodded my head.

"Crowne Plaza."

Malik beeped in.

"Meet me outside."

"We're out there."

Me and De went upstairs. Workers are setting up the club for the night. It must be eight o'clock. I called Imani's number from the cell. Still nothing. I paged her two-way. Me and De walked through the club and stood out front. I put my foot up against the wall. Malik jumped out of his whip and walked up.

"Feds rushed Tony's spot. They got the Benz."

"Damn," I said.

"It's more to it," Malik said. He lit a cigarette. "They say they got flicks of me pushing that bitch."

"What the fuck is up," De said. "When did a camera come in to play?"

"Joey ain't a professional like that," Malik said.

"But he got cops on his team," I said. "Yo hunt this dude down so I can kill him."

"Damn gangster," Malik said. "This must be personal you gunning and shit."

"It's always about business," De said from my left. "Let's set this shit off."

De took his phone out of his pocket.

"Monster."

"Holla."

"Get with me."

"Ten minutes."

"You got this," I said. "Hit me up when shit change. You know where I'll be."

I walked over to my ride and boned out to Imani's crib. I got like no seconds to find her. I am so serious. I walked in the crib at nine and called Destiny's room with the quickness.

"Good evening."

"Destiny it's Q."

"What's up brother?"

"I'm cool. What's good with you?"

"It's all good. Politics as usual. Is Imani with you?"

"Y'all ain't link up today?"

Tell me something good.

"We were supposed to hit up Cherrywood and buy the mall out. But she ain't come through."

Shit.

"I'll let her know you called."

"Q you called me. What's…"

I hung up before she could say shit else. Imani in all of this missing in action bullshit ain't sitting well with me. I'm slipping. I sat in the darkness. Somebody rang the bell.

"Who that?"

"Detective Price."

"Are you by yourself?"

"Aren't you? Open the door."

I buzzed the door and Jovan came up. I turned on the lights.

"What's up?"

I stood in the middle of the floor.

"I've been watching you for a while and shit doesn't look good."

"I never had time for your petty ass games. The set don't change. What up?"

"You're right we are meeting under antagonistic conditions. Joseph Stanton, Andre Thomas, and Keith Williams. Two are badges."

"You just figured that out," I said. "About fucking time."

"Quinnzel they have Imani and they will kill her, but right now she's their only insurance."

"Fuck you talking about man?"

"Imani did some things for me which led me to Joey. Coinciding with an in-house internal affairs investigation throwing Thomas and Williams all up in your project."

"So this is your fault."

"You are as much to blame. Imani would die for you and you gave her the gun."

"Jovan…"

"No you listen. A car was stolen from the property of a Ms. Asia Simms by this man."

Jovan pulled out a picture of Malik.

"Do you know who this man was last seen with? This man."

She pulled out a picture and gave it to me. It's me.

"Do you know what was found in the trunk? This man."

She didn't pull out another picture.

"You know what man it is. Good news is the car isn't registered to you. Bad news is our only witness died in a fire chained to a bed."

"Who?"

"Asia Simms stupid," Jovan said. "She was Andre's former fiancée. Lucky for you the shit is blowing in another direction."

"Fuck all that. They got my woman. Fuck is the deal?"

"The bust at the docks, drug related killings dating back some time ago."

"Why are you telling me all of this? I have one concern."

"To stick it to them. That's why Imani was helping me, to clear your name of all suspicions."

I stepped back and rubbed my hands over my face.

"What I got to do?"

"Joey lays low. Where?"

"DoubleTree Hotel. Hold. I got a key."

I went to the closet and pulled out my Polo jacket. I checked the pocket.

"It's not here."

"Could Imani have gotten a hold of it? She's a mighty hunter."

"Now she's the prey."

"Quinnzel we are going to get her back. You have to believe that."

"I hear you. Check her briefcase it's by the counter."

Jovan turned around and looked behind her.

"No, it's not."

I shook my head.

"Fuck."

"I'll check Imani's office. I need you to stay here by this phone in case she calls."

"You crazy."

"Quinnzel you…"

"I'm not trying to hear you. This nigga done drew and…"

"And if you act without means you will lose her. Please let me do my job. I'm good at it."

"Alright. But if you ain't got shit by midnight, I'm killing somebody."

Imani

I lay with my hands chained to a bed stripped down to my Victoria Secrets. The room is spinning out of control and I can't see. I'm blindfolded. I can't get my balance. My mind is foggy. My lip feels swollen but I can't touch it. I used my tongue only to taste my blood. Shit where am I. Who am I with? A million questions with no one to answer. Or is it? I held my breath to see if I could hear someone else breathing. I don't hear shit. The last thing I remember is…damn it, I don't remember. I don't even know how long I've been here. I came home from my dad's house on Sunday night. Shit, I must've been drugged. And with all of the crazy fuck your ass up beam you up to Scottie narcotics floating around these days who the fuck knows what's in my system. My body feels weak and I'm exhausted. I feel shitty all over. I'm actually glad I'm filthy and for the first time in my life I hope my pussy smells like feet and corn chips.

I hear voices approaching. A door opened and closed. Weed stench filled the air.

"That bitch got the fucking car," one voice said.

It doesn't sound familiar but it is a male voice. Who's he talking to?

"And they'll be on our asses by sunset," a different voice said. "The clock is ticking. Let's get it together."

"We got something they want," a third voice said. "Chill regular."

It's Joey. Oh shit. I felt weight shift on the bed and a hand on my thigh. I kicked my leg.

"Get the fuck off of me," I said through tightened jaws.

"You got a lot of fire in your ass," Joey said. He pulled my blindfold down. "You best watch your mouth, I'm from the tribe of smack a ho."

I surveyed my surroundings. Hotel room. It has to be the DoubleTree. I never saw the other guys before. Joey sat on top of me. He tried to kiss me but I turned my face. He bitch slapped me with his backhand. The sting on my cheek made my eyes water but I damn sure ain't shed a tear.

"You brought it on yourself," Joey said. "I knew Supreme was your dude. I ain't stupid. You tried to run your little game smooth and shit. Now look at you.

He laughed.

"This is a big boy league you should be watching from the sidelines. Matter of fact you ain't worthy of the sidelines. You deserve the nose bleed seats. You're the one who isn't ready. But I got something for that ass."

Joey leaned his body down on mine.

"You all teary eyed and shit," he said. "Get your shit together ebony eyes."

Joey licked my cheek.

"Dre," he said. "Get that bitch on the horn. Tell her if she don't back the fuck up, Ms. Imani here will be mailed back to her ass piece by piece."

Dre laughed.

"Not before I get a ride on that sweet shit," he said.

He pulled a cell phone from his jacket pocket and went in the hallway.

"Come on J," the other dude said. "We ain't got time to be bullshitting."

Joey jumped up off of the bed and got in his face.

"What is you scared nigga, get a dog." Joey pulled a gun out of his waistband and stuck it in dude's mouth. "I run this shit. You don't do or say shit until I point to you."

Dude raised his hands and nodded his head.

"Now sit your five dollar ass down before I make change," Joey said. He turned and looked at me smiling. "I always wanted to say that shit."

He came back over to the bed and sat down. Joey ran the barrel of the gun across the top of my breasts.

"Damn girl. You eat wheaties don't you?"

Dre came back in the room.

"J they got APB's out on us," he said. "With assistance from the State Troopers."

"Excellent," Joey said. "The more the fucking merrier."

He's bugged the fuck out.

"Fuck Price," Joey said. "Get my message to the chief of muthafucking police. Lady hoops is my hostage and shit ain't moving until I say so. Tell them big J sent you."

Damn when all you got is nothing, nobody to care for nobody to love you, there is no difference between life and death. I asked Joey about his peoples while we were out those nights. He said his mom is a crack head, pop is a no show, and his sister is out there, way the fuck out there. And he said it with no remorse like it didn't bother him one bit. He said being alone made him stronger, that he showed everyone he could amount to something all by himself. With no one to raise him and teach him he basically amounts to shit. A weak ass brother who takes joy in bringing other people misery because pain is all he knows. I feel sorry for him. Too many boys grow up to be nothing niggas behind a household of demise. They don't know any better. And if they do they don't give a fuck because life ain't worth living to them in a society that gives them it's ass to kiss. Damn black America. We need to unite for our children's sake. Save our children from this type of struggle. Peace and unity amongst brothers will be our sole source of survival. Please believe me. Joey pushed my blindfold up and kissed my lips.

"I love you," he said. "Keith watch her. Dre, come with me."

He got up and I heard a door close.

"Are you okay," Keith said.

"Like you really give a fuck."

"You must be hungry."

I heard him approach. I felt for his extended hand and smacked whatever was in it to the floor.

"I don't want shit from you."

I heard a cell phone ring and Keith's voice retreat. A door opened and closed and another door opened. I didn't hear it shut.

"What the fuck are you doing," Keith said.

It sounds like he's standing right over me.

"Fuck does it look like I'm doing?"

He pulled my blindfold down. I blinked my eyes to gain focus. He looked around the room.

"J," he said. "Andre?"

A red dot flashed on Keith's back. My eyes followed the beam to the bathroom. I held my composure so he wouldn't suspect anything.

"Did you hear something," Keith said.

I heard two shots fired.

"Shut the fuck up. You're under arrest."

Keith fell forward on the bed. His dead weight hovered on my legs. I turned around. Jovan emerged from the bathroom.

"Where did you come from," I said.

"Shower," she said smiling. "You ready?"

Quinnzell Supreme Sharpe

I let a week go by and I'm still experiencing some madness. This muthafucking nigga Joey flipped the fuck out and abducted my Queen. Held her captive against her will and shit. My lady's safe, now it's on. Niggas got the scope out for that nigga as we speak. He's been on the run since Jovan put the clamp down. Imani, her ass is restricted to soft mattresses and fluffy pillows under my supervision because I said so. I'm keeping her hemmed up at my crib until further fucking notice. She has to go to Atlanta tomorrow to bang microphones with Charles Barkley and blaze the airwaves. Once her plane touches back in Philly its back to the drill again. I'm not fucking playing. Joey got to get dealt with, pulling the shit he did. It's off with his muthafucking head early. On some no hold barred shit. I'll show him how to do this son.

Imani turned over and put her arm around me. I kissed her forehead and moved her hair from her face. I'm going to chill a little something because I know she's safe, sleeping beside me. I'm trying to put a bug in her ear to make her stay here, yamean. Fuck it. She can buss out her work from here. Route all of that office shit straight to this muthafucka. No problem. I'm a see what it is, yamean. Do whatever I have to do to keep my Queen protected. I told y'all that's how puss niggas get down; they come at your Queen to break your back. It ain't about shit because I'm coming at Joey's neck until he's fucking dead. And until then he ain't safe, his momma and them ain't safe, the fucking roaches in his crib ain't safe. Niggas want to act, we can act. I called all cars on this one. Soon as somebody get the drop on that nigga it's off with his fucking head. No question, no rap.

We're going to hit that nigga free fall while everybody's rumbling. Shit if you can freestyle you can spit off air early. I'm tired as shit but I ain't even worried about sleeping until I know that nigga can't get up. And if we don't get this nigga by the morning we're running up in his moms' house. Fuck that. What goes around comes back the fuck around. Off niggas in his fam from the front of the line until Joey's ass fall flat line. I didn't want it to come to this but it will be what it is. It's all written, I'm just playing my part.

De knocked on my bedroom door. I got up and wrapped a sheet around me.

"What up Money?"

"We got him dog. Get dressed."

I closed the door and blew out the candles. Imani sat up.

"Quinnzel I need you. Everyday I need you," Imani said with tears in her eyes. "Babe don't go. Fuck this shit, fuck dude. I'm saying."

I ain't say shit. I went to my dresser and put my boxers on.

"Quinnzel, let's just be out you and me. Please let's just go."

"Imani don't do this alright." I put my socks on and pulled my sweat pants up. "You know what it is."

"I don't know shit. What is it Q?"

"I got to handle myself."

"Babe, it's over just walk away. Please hear me."

"I can't."

"Can't you? You can or you won't because you can if you want to. You always have a choice. Life is what you make it."

"Fuck it, I'm not. Sound good to you."

"Why Q?"

I sat on the bed with my back to Imani.

"I have to protect my family. If niggas think they can run in and snatch my peoples up or do whatever and its gravy, I'm a mark forever. I'm not living like that."

"Quinnzel it's not that serious."

"It is fucking serious. Aren't you a college student, add this shit up and you tell me what it is. I know what I'm about and I'm not a fucking sucker for niggas to be coming at me anyway they feel. Yamean, earn respect."

"I respect you."

"This isn't about you."

"So that was you chained up like a fucking slave. My bad."

"Imani…"

"Never mind Quinnzel. We're back to being strangers. Do you okay?"

I laced up my boots.

"I'll be back in the morning to take you to the airport. Get some sleep."

"Whatever."

Imani laid down and threw the covers up over her face. I grabbed my black RocaWear sweatshirt and met De out back.

I got fucked up on the drive to Philly piping myself up to dead this nigga. De boned out on the highway. Malik hit me up on my two-way and said they were on the move following that nigga to wherever he stops. I loaded all of my clips and you know it's always one in the chamber. Malik hit me up and said they followed him past the Place. That's a bar in the cuts back Eastside. I told him to stay on that nigga. We're eating the road up on some quick shit but we can't get there fast enough. Malik hit me up on a three-piece saying they're at Palmers the after hours spot. I'm like we'll be there in a minute. We met Malik on a dark ass side street behind the club. He had some stocky niggas with him ready to bang dope.

"Yo Supreme," Malik said. "You ain't hit up the professional. You ready to put a hole in a muthafucka."

"Let's do this," I said. "Who is he with?"

"Four niggas," Malik said.

"We'll rush his team," De said. "Q handle your shit."

"No muthafucking doubt," I said.

"Yo, we going to go up in the club blasting," Malik said.

"Hell yeah," one of the dudes with him said.

"Fuck no," De said. "Go find me a bitch. Matter of fact. Hold up."

De went around to the front of the club. I sat on the hood stressing. I need to get my mind right. It ain't no turning back from this shit. But I got to do what I got to do. Niggas coming after my Queen I'm not having it. I don't have a choice.

"Supreme you straight," Malik said.

"Yeah nigga. I'm cool."

I'm shitting bricks but I'm cool. De walked back around the corner.

"Alright the jawn is going to sweet talk his ass and make him come outside," De said. "Knowing him, he won't come out on the solo."

"What's her move," Malik said.

"Dome in the whip," De said. "He won't say no."

"Let's roll to the front," I said. "At first sight open fire like Elmer Fudd in duck season."

The niggas walked around the corner. De held me up.

"Baby boss you got this?"

"I'm doing what I got to."

De hugged me.

"Alright my nigga. I got your back but you the man."

"Let's work."

Me and De walked around front. De looked for his pawn.

"Move," De said when he saw her.

Joey and his team stepped outside. Shit is moving at the speed of light but seemed like it was stuck in slow motion. Mad shots sprayed all over. Bystanders ducking, falling, jumping over shit. I licked shots at Joey aiming for his head. I bust my guns on target and watched that nigga fall. My third eye seen it coming before it happened. Fire penetrated my body. Bullets branded my chest opening holes.

"De, I'm hit."

I'm not ready to die. I got too much living to do.

"Mommy I love you. Imani I'm sorry."

I hear Him coming.

"God forgive me."

Imani

My bedside is cold. Quinnzel rolled his punk ass out anyway last night. It's cool, I ain't hardly tripping. To call a truce he'll come home to a banquet sized breakfast; Pancakes, eggs, grits, bacon. And the orange juice stays freshly squeezed on the morning basis. Maybe I'll break out the Belgian waffle maker and put it down like that. Hell yeah. That's what I'm talking about. Betty Crocker got my number on speed dial talking about can she get a hook up. The skills are crucial. I sat up and stretched. A red velvet ring box with gold trimming lay like a whisper on my pillow. Damn, is this his way of proposing?

Visit amazon.com or your local bookstore